Love Knows No Boundaries

Coffee

**Lock Down Publications
Presents
Love Knows No Boundaries
A Novel by *Coffee***

Lock Down Publications
P.O. Box 870494
Mesquite, Tx 75187

Visit our website at www.lockdownpublications.com

First Edition May 2014
Revised Edition January 2015
Printed in the United States of America

This is a work of fiction. Names, characters, places, and incidents either are products of the author's imagination or are used fictitiously. Any similarity to actual events or locales or persons, living or dead, is entirely coincidental.

Cover design and layout by: **Dynasty's Cover Me**
Book interior design by: **Shawn Walker**
Edited by: **Shawn Walker**

Stay Connected with Us!

Text **LOCKDOWN** to 22828 to stay up-to-date with new releases, sneak peaks, contests and more…

Thank you!

Submission Guideline.

Submit the first three chapters of your completed manuscript to ldpsubmissions@gmail.com, subject line: Your book's title. The manuscript must be in a .doc file and sent as an attachment. Document should be in Times New Roman, double spaced and in size 12 font. Also, provide your synopsis and full contact information. If sending multiple submissions, they must each be in a separate email.

Have a story but no way to send it electronically? You can still submit to LDP/Ca$h Presents. Send in the first three chapters, written or typed, of your completed manuscript to:

LDP: Submissions Dept
Po Box 1482
Pine Lake, Ga 30072

DO NOT send original manuscript. Must be a duplicate.

Provide your synopsis and a cover letter containing your full contact information.

Thanks for considering LDP and Ca$h Presents.

~Dedication~

To my parents, **Emile and Mary**, every day of my life is dedicated to reflecting all of the soul food that you've fed me over the years. May I leave an imprint on the lives I encounter the way you two have done with me, so generously. I love you two, more than words can say.

To **my rock**, what's understood doesn't need to be explained.

Coffee

Chapter 1

"**A**re you sure you're ready for this day?" Samiyah asked Minnie, staring her squarely in the eyes with the attempt to gauge her response.

"Yes, I am pos-o-tive." She happily stated before taking a more serious tone. "I've never felt more certain about anyone in my life." Minnie twirled around in the Cheval mirror, trying to hide her imperfections.

Samiyah thought briefly before cutting to the chase. "I'm not trying to be cynical, but don't you think that one year is too soon to be marrying somebody?" Minnie's husband-to-be rubbed her wrong.

"*Really?*" she grimaced. "*Today?*" Sarcasm trickled from her question. "Don't you think *six* years is too long to not have married Gerran?" Minnie reversed the interrogation on Samiyah's relationship. "You may feel some type of way about G'Corey, but I can vouch for him so you'll just have to trust me." She sat down, offered her best friend of fifteen years a seat beside her, then reached out and held Samiyah's hand. "You can be so protective at times, but I'm not as naïve as you think."

"But y'all are so different in the ways that matter most. I feel like you're an easier prey to someone like him and you know I've never made my suspicions secret, so don't give me that look." Samiyah mirrored the twisted expression on Minnie's face. "All I wanted to do was ask my sister one last time before I finalize this subject for good," she stressed. "Of all the men you can possibly settle down with, he's the one you choose?"

"What *men?*" She huffed in amusement. "Listen, Yah, my intelligence is sexy, my face is pretty, even my conversation is intriguing, once you get to know me, but my body doesn't just snatch a man's attention, so my pickings are slim."

9

"So, you're settling?" Samiyah questioned and Minnie's eyes drew inward. "That came out wrong. You're all that." Minnie was about to protest, but Samiyah stopped her. "You don't have to be five-ten and thin."

"I agree, but that's easy for you to say. You don't mirror my issues. Look at you." She outlined Samiyah's shape, "You're fine as wine, but me," she grabbed at her double mid-section, "I'm five-one and bigger than I care to share."

"When a man loves a woman, he sees past her hang-ups. G'Corey isn't the only *or* the best one," she added. "We both know the man you should be with is—"

"Enough, Yah!" Minnie demanded as she rose to her feet, "I love *him!*" she affirmed. "And just because I'm not the lioness you want me to be, doesn't make me a kitten either." Minnie walked over to the opened window to feel the summer breeze wisp against her heated skin.

Samiyah rationalized that objecting yet again would, for certain, turn ugly so she zipped her lips and locked that matter away as she said she would. She picked up a napkin and called out Minnie's name, getting her attention. She waved it in the air as if it were a white flag.

Charmingly, Minnie smiled. Samiyah did the same. They walked toward each other and hugged instinctually.

"I love you, girl," Samiyah whispered in her ear.

"I love you too, Yah."

Comfortable silence fell between them briefly.

"What time do you have?" Minnie broke their embrace.

Samiyah looked at her cell phone, "It's five—nineteen."

"Do you know where Acacia and Kawanna are? They should have been back already."

"No idea," she answered. "Should I find them?"

"It would be nice to have all my girls with me as I prepare to be Mrs. Daniels. Ooh," she closed her eyes sweetly, "I *love* the sound of that."

Without a rebuttal, Samiyah turned on her heels and then headed out of the door to find the missing bridesmaids.

***

Immediately stepping out of the prep room, Samiyah ran into Acacia, the Puerto Rican bombshell as well as *her* boyfriend, Sleepy.

"Que pasa? I was just about to look for you." Samiyah dapped her girl off. "Hey, Sleepy," she casually waved. He nodded in a swift upward motion. Acacia stood snuggly against him with her arm interlocking his, picking barely seen lint off of his tuxedo. "Where is Kawanna?"

"Don't know. Don't care." Acacia said boldly while tracing the outline of her petite frame as if to suggest that her presence was enough. "Damn her! I don't know why she's even in the wedding to begin with. She isn't Minnie's real friend anyway."

"You and I know that, but this isn't about us," Samiyah reminded her.

Acacia rolled her eyes, "I guess."

"Listen, I wanna talk to you," she lowered her tone, raising her eyebrows, "in private. Come with me to find her and I'll explain." Samiyah gently tugged at her arm.

Acacia huffed in disgust. Her unwillingness to go with Samiyah flashed across her face before she could fix her mouth to say *no*. She had zero intentions on leaving Sleepy's side.

He was the spitting image of Adam Rodriquez, the sexy Latin detective from CSI Miami, with the exception of his natural low gaze which was how he earned his nickname, Sleepy.

With all the women in attendance, there was no way she'd leave him alone. "We can talk later. Besides, that's not a two man hunt."

11

"Go with your friend." Sleepy warmly suggested after surveying the urgency in Samiyah's request.

"Why?" she erupted as she cut her eyes in his direction. "You want to be by yourself so you can do something you got no business doing?" she spoke accusatorily.

"No, Acacia!" he frowned.

"So, why you tryna ditch me?"

He dropped his head then shook it in disbelief. Her quickness to make mountains of mole hills was a thorn in his side. She bombarded him with questions in rapid succession. He looked at her sternly, silent still, before walking away.

"Sleep—," Acacia said sharply. She found herself quickly flushed with frustration from his dismissive attitude. "Oooh," her lips curled. She was moments away from putting one foot in front of the other to march behind him, but Samiyah jumped in front of her to block her path.

"Acacia," she snapped her fingers in her face. "You just got your man back. Chill out. He ain't goin' nowhere. Damn!"

"I'm supposed to walk on eggshells because he came back? Oh, no!" She rolled her neck. "That's even more reason to be on that behind. There are too many piranhas coming in and out of this church for me to chill."

"Look at me," Samiyah whirled her finger clockwise in front of her own face. "I need you. So come with me. Ahora!"

Samiyah slipped her arm around Acacia's to lead her away. Acacia aversely followed, "Alright. But this *can't* take long."

***

"On my *wedding day*?" He looked at her suspiciously. "Are you nuts?" He surveyed that she was unmoved by his questions. And before she could answer, he followed up with another. "You're serious aren't you?"

"You already know I am." She flashed a devilish grin then beckoned him to follow her into one of the unused church rooms with a quick wave of her hand. She walked in first and then he looked around to see if anyone was in sight before he stepped in behind her. "This is wild!"

She licked her lips. "Leaving the door wide open is wild," she secured the lock. "We're safe. Now let me unzip you," she tugged at his pants.

"Don't make a mess on my tux," he stated as she secured a spot on her knees.

"Do I ever make a mess?" She inquired lustfully as she took the liberty of freeing his manhood from his boxers.

"You my kinda bitch, ya heard me." He moaned as he wrapped his hands in her hair and enjoyed his Australian kiss, *the kiss down under.*

* * *

After twenty minutes of scouting the church grounds both in and out, they saw who they were looking for. "There she is." Both Acacia and Samiyah said simultaneously once they spotted Kawanna walking.

Acacia abruptly stopped inches short of her and folded her arms. "Where have you been? We have been looking for your..." she paused before she slipped and cursed in the Lord's house, "...tail."

"'Scuse you!" Kawanna stumbled over her words. She was shocked that she was being charged up by a woman she only knew through association.

"No need for the glares ladies," Samiyah calmly stated, noticing that Kawanna had become defensive.

"Check yo friend!" Kawanna hissed.

Before Acacia could say a peep Samiyah hammered, "Nah, check yo' self! And while you're at it, pretend we like each other, at least for today."

Kawanna cut her eyes at them both. "Whatever," she replied dismissively as she moved past them.

"Tu pelo parece como mierda," Kawanna knew Acacia was shit stirring, but she paid her no never mind as she continued her stride.

"What did you just say?" Samiyah chuckled at Acacia's expression.

With much annoyance she blurted, "I said her hair looks like *ca ca.*"

Samiyah shook her head and laughed before she took off in the same direction as Kawanna.

Following suit, Acacia hunched her shoulders, "Well it does."

***

Minutes before the wedding and now you call? Samiyah thought as she shook her head and placed her phone back into her purse.

Gerran was supposed to escort her down the aisle as the best man, but now she would have to improvise.

The wedding planner was finalizing the ends and outs as she coordinated their places. "Where is…," she fumbled through the list on her clipboard. "…Gerran? I didn't see him amongst the men."

"He won't be making it," Samiyah sweetly smiled to conceal her truest feeling of aggravation.

"What?" The lady stammered.

"Humph," Kawanna snickered.

"The hell?" Acacia commented at Kawanna's snide remark.

"Why?" Minnie asked fretfully, fanning her eyes to prevent the welling tears from ruining her makeup.

Samiyah looked at Minnie and mouthed, *I'm sorry.* She then turned to the coordinator, "I'll just have to make walking solo look fabulous."

The planner sighed then smiled in an effort to keep Minnie calm, "The beat goes on," she peppered up. "You stay here. I will be back to get you," she advised the bride. "Come, ladies." She opened the door for the women to exit.

Less than half an hour later the pastor concluded the ceremony. "…by the power vested in me by the state of Louisiana. I now pronounce you husband and wife."

Coffee

Chapter 2

Everyone arrived at the hall for the reception and was greeted with the sound of the Lil Rascals Brass Band. Random people walking nearby had to pay homage to the celebratory music with a few dance steps of their own. It was a party on the outside before getting to the party on the inside. Everybody threw their hands up, skipped, dipped and swayed in a second line fashion as they entered. No rehearsal. Just an instinct from growing up in the Crescent City.

After the song ended and all the guests were indoors, G'Corey stood on the platform and called for everyone's focus. First, he thanked Minnie for her hand in marriage.

"Bluh." Samiyah made a gag expression as if she threw up when she heard his speech. The sincerity of his words were clouded by her distrust.

Acacia elbowed her slightly in her side. "Be nice," her brows furrowed.

Samiyah turned to her and mouthed, *Okay*. They both chuckled.

Choosing to tune him out, Samiyah noticed everything was tastefully decorated black and gold. A clear representation of the *five-oh-fo*. They spared no expense and that was obvious from the elaborate wedding to the exquisite hall.

"Enough of me talking, ya heard me." G'Corey kissed his wife then raised a glass of Hennessey in the air. "Laissez les bon temps roulez," he said, using the Cajun expression which means: Let the good times roll. And on that note, the crowd erupted in cheers and did just that.

Samiyah ventured away from the throng of people to check her phone that had been relentlessly vibrating inside of her clutch. The string of ignored calls and text messages were from Gerran.

3:53PM: You don't want to know why I can't make it to the wedding?
6:07PM: I don't have time for your shit! You know I'm sorry.
7:39PM: Answer your damn phone!

"When I get good and goddamn ready," Samiyah sassily spoke at the phone before putting it away.

Suddenly she felt a pair of strong hands grabbing her waist from behind, surprising her as she nearly jumped out of her skin. She turned around.

"Elias!" She belted, slapping him against his chest. "Boy, you scared me."

"Thought it was somebody else?" he spoke in a smooth as butter tone.

"No. You just startled me, that's all," she wrapped her arms around his neck as his Prada cologne wafted up her nostrils.

Samiyah stood back and examined his attire. "You look so debonair," she admired how G'Q'd he was.

He wore an Armani all-black three piece suit with a pair of black Ferragamo Crocs.

"You know you stunning too, bay-bae," he complimented. Samiyah smiled.

Elias bobbed his head to the music as his eyes darted from one end of the hall to the next. "I spotted the happy couple, but where is Fatal Attraction and her vic'?" he referred to Acacia and Sleepy's strange relationship.

"A mess," she laughed. "They're over there ducked off in the corner," Samiyah pointed.

"She a hot mess," he smirked. "I see Gerran didn't make it *again.*"

Samiyah said nothing and Elias knew that to mean she was good on discussing the topic.

As Kenny Latimore's song *For You* saturated the building, she almost wondered what it would be like to dance to her own wedding tune. But soon after the selection ended, so did her thoughts. The throwback bounce rap *Buck Jump Time* by Gregory D started bouncing off of the walls. It was just the jam to get the party started.

"Come on, Elias, that's my shit," she called out, using her hand like a megaphone, "dance with me."

"But what will the females think, seeing me freakin' you on tha floor?" He bit his lip, grinding the thin air with his hands stretched out in front of him like he was holding onto a jumbo booty for demonstration.

She burst out laughing, "Shut up, boy, and come on. A ho is a ho, they'll want you regardless."

"You ain't never lied."

She popped and dipped to the sounds blaring from the speakers in true New Orleans style. Elias kept up but with less energy than what Samiyah was bringing.

They danced to four songs straight before she got tired. "Whoo, I need a break. These heels are killing me," she agonized. "I'm gonna chill for a second."

"Do ya thing. I'll be around."

Samiyah walked over to the bar and leaned slightly over the partition as she waited her turn for service.

"And what will you have?" The bartender asked in the sexiest of tones.

Oh, my, she took notice. He was sinfully fine. She closed her eyes hard and unusually long before she opened them. *Yep, still fine*, she thought.

She flirted back. "You, if you weren't working, but a coke will do."

He flashed a quick smile, showcasing twelve shiny gold teeth placed perfectly between a set of juicy, full lips. "Here you go, boo,"

19

he chuckled as he handed her the beverage. "Don't forget your napkin," he insinuated that she look at it.

She took her drink without unlocking their gaze. His smile caught her off guard again. *Damn!* She nodded at the bartender who never stopped watching her. Slowly, she strolled over to her seat at the wedding party's table.

She grabbed her phone and sent a short text to Cedric.

8:35PM: He didn't. You should have.

He replied.

8:36PM: I still can.

She didn't respond. She simply allowed the smile to marinate on her face.

Samiyah glanced over at the bar again. The bartender, who was still watching her, held napkins in the air and then pointed toward hers. She motioned her head, acknowledging his request. She flipped her napkin over, read it and then walked over to Elias who was grinding on a slender cutie.

Samiyah tapped his shoulder, "Read this."

He backed off of the female he was on, still moving but at a slower pace.

Get off in half an hour. Meet me at the gazebo out back... Brian

He glanced at her, "So what's the verdict?"

"I don't know." She peeked over at Brian once more.

"You single tonight, so do ya thing, Slick. I ain't mad atcha," he smiled.

They chuckled at the thought, then Elias stopped dancing altogether and walked off with Samiyah. The girl folded her arms in disgust at his abrupt dismissal but she walked away quietly.

Minnie danced in place, showing off her three carat marquis cut diamond. Everyone hugged and congratulated the couple with the exception of Samiyah who was very much standoffish. Minnie was so lost in her moment she didn't pay her friend's reserve any mind.

"Aren't you gonna congratulate Minnie?" Acacia asked.

"What for? I don't see anything good about those two being official."

"Yea, you do," Acacia pointed at Minnie. "You see that smile plastered on her face? That came from within. Mr. Right or Mr. Wrong, G'Corey makes her happy. Celebrate that."

Acacia was ruled by her emotions. Oftentimes that got her into trouble, but at that moment it helped her make perfect sense. Samiyah yet again placed her feelings on the back burner, embraced Minnie and commemorated her joy, but not the occasion.

"Samiyah? Samiyah?" Elias snapped his long fingers in front of her face. "It's past that time," he tapped his watch.

"Oh," she brought herself into the now.

"And what time is that?" Minnie asked as Acacia cosigned.

Samiyah scurried away, talking above the music, "I'll tell y'all later."

***

"I thought you weren't coming," Brian patted the space next to him for Samiyah to sit.

"And what made you think that?"

"I have been waiting out c'here with no sign of you for a good," he twisted his watch toward his face, "ten minutes."

"That's because I debated whether or not I should meet you," she spoke directly.

"And why the hesitation? You gotta man?"

"Actually, I do. *I shouldn't claim his ass,* she thought.

"Well, there's no harm in conversation—is there?"

"As good as you look and as alone as I feel, I wouldn't *conversate* for too long. But I actually came because I didn't want to stand you up," she twirled a few of his chest length dreads between her fingers. "But I gotta go," she determined.

21

"Just like that?" he questioned, looking like he regretted her decision.

She nodded her head *yes*, "Just like that." She could have used the company, but her vulnerability was too high for their encounter to be casual only. She bit her lip to prevent herself from speaking as she stood to her feet and began walking away, slowly. Otherwise, she would be sexing him on the spot.

"Can I at least know your name?"

She playfully turned toward him, "It's a secret."

He diminished the few feet that separated them. He smelled so good her knees buckled. He scribbled his number on a piece of paper and cupped it in her hand.

"If you ever want to reveal that secret," he eyed her seductively, "or Victoria's *secret*," he kissed her hand with those soft lips that felt better against her skin than she imagined, "call me, ya heard me."

She extracted her hand from his slowly, "Maybe." His persistence was an aphrodisiac and if he said one more thing. Just one more thing, she was going to surrender the goods.

"Stay sexy—Secret," he watched the swing of her hips as she reentered the building.

***

"You straight?" Eli asked the moment he saw her.

She flipped her hand side to side to indicate she felt so. "I came *that* close to giving in." She pinched her fingers together in front of her eye.

"It wouldn't have been a second thought for me. Carpe diem, my sista. *Carpe diem*."

He threw his arm around her shoulder and walked with her over to their friends who were soon departing.

Acacia kissed Minnie and wished her well on her honeymoon. She then pecked Samiyah on her cheek while whispering in her ear. "Tell me what you skipped off to do."

"Wasn't nothing," Samiyah admitted.

"I'm sure," Acacia stated in a disbelieving manner.

"Bye, girl," she waved Acacia off. Samiyah walked over and hugged Minnie, "Enjoy yourself."

"You mean that?" Minnie questioned her genuineness. "It would mean the world if you do because I want you to be happy for me."

She drew an X over her heart, "I do. I've chaptered that issue as promised."

Minnie smiled brightly then returned to her husband in an almost skip kind of saunter.

Samiyah bid her adieus to those who remained. "I'm out this piece." She threw up two fingers like Martin Payne, "Peaceeeeee."

Elias walked her to her car and decided he was ready as well. "A'ight, peoples. I'm 'bout to bounce myself. I have someone to get into." He rubbed his hands together in a maniacal manner. "Get home safe. Love you."

"Love you too, bow wow."

23

Coffee

Chapter 3

The sunlight peered through the semi-parted blinds of Samiyah's bedroom, forcing her eyes to open with struggle.

"Umm," she stretched her arms above her head as she kicked one of her legs out from underneath the comforter of her king sized bed. Her home phone began ringing and she knew without checking the caller I.D. who it was. She rubbed her eyes to focus on the time that flashed 9:18AM on her nightstand before she answered. "Hello."

"Hello, huh?" Gerran breathed fire into the receiver. "Why the hell didn't you call me?"

"Good morning to you, too." She slowly sat up in her bed. Sleep was present in her voice.

"Your answer?" He remarked without pleasantries.

"Hold on," she spoke curtly as indignation woke her fully. "Don't check me like you have a leg to stand on. I wouldn't have had a call to ignore from you if you were there like you were supposed to be."

"You never want to—" Gerran barged into her spiel.

"Unh—unh. Let me finish," Samiyah admonished. "As if playing me wasn't bad enough, you let Minnie down too. You were the best man in her wedding. A *wedding*," she reiterated, "you committed to months ago. So, to answer your question, I ignored all your calls because I didn't want to hear what would be another excuse as to why you couldn't make time for me!"

"So, you decided to have a tantrum instead of finding out the deal?"

"Every action has a what, Gerran?" she asked rhetorically. "We can do this all day, but no matter how you slice it, you were wrong!"

"A'ight. I'll take my charge on this one." He blew her off.

"That's not an apology," she made clear.

He sighed, "I'm sorry. It wasn't my intention to stand you up or ruin anything for Minnie," he humbled himself.

Samiyah simmered as well. "And *you're* right. I shouldn't have disregarded you. It just pissed me off to take yet *another* backseat. I'm so tired of being alone in this relationship," she complained.

Business had to be handled but her pleading tone spoke volumes and Gerran couldn't turn a deaf ear to it. "How about you meet me at my house? We can do breakfast at the Trolley Stop. It doesn't make up for yesterday, but it's an olive branch nonetheless," Gerran offered.

"I'd like that, but no games," she softly advised. "I'll be there in a minute."

***

"You weren't playin' when you said a minute." Gerran leaned down to kiss Samiyah, then removed the lip gloss that was impressed upon his lips.

"Of course I wasn't, I barely get time to leisurely see you these days.

Gerran looked in Samiyah's direction. "Well, I'm ready to eat."

"You're not even dressed." She walked over to his closet with the intentions of picking out an outfit for him, hoping he wasn't about to renege on their plans.

"For starters, you have on too many clothes for where I want to grub at?" He expressed as he stood before her with an erection poking through the slit of his boxers.

"Hmmm, I see. *I'm* what's on the menu?"

Without hesitation, he removed his boxers so she could see him fully. She always admired looking at his muscular, caramel physique. He stood six feet, three inches towering over her five feet, seven inch stature, which made him an Adonis to her.

Physically, he was the picture of perfection. Mentally, he was focused like a predator on a kill excursion, but his sexual delivery plummeted in her mind when his energies communicated she was on his check list of *things to do*. That made sex more strategic than romantic.

There was no more time for excitement, just getting down to brass tacks.

She loved him despite their challenges, but she hated the theatrics. Faking orgasms were bad but having to inconspicuously moisten her dry vagina presented its challenges above all. His inattentiveness definitely took a toll on their love life.

But Gerran was worth the drama to Samiyah because no matter how good the sexual chemistry was between herself and others, she knew he would always provide, love, and stay down for her. That made for a good husband one day.

She reminded herself of that as he tugged at her purple panties.

He placed her on top of his kitchen table, removed her undies and indulged in her sweet delight. She gyrated her hips trying to help him find her *ooh wee* spot so it wouldn't be a complete waste, but it was to no avail.

The ache from his throbbing flesh commanded he enter her, and that he did. His penetration was her cue to begin the charade of satisfaction. She may have been wrong to deceive him, but she couldn't damage his ego. So, she matched his whimpers until he came and then just like that, in a matter of minutes, it was over.

"Breakfast smelled as good as it tasted," Gerran sniffed her underwear and then looked at his phone as a calendar reminder made it chime.

"Hand me my panties, so I can get dressed. You get dressed, too." She snatched them from his hands.

"About that," he checked his watch. "I will have to write you a rain check. I completely forgot about this appointment I have scheduled. I could delay what I was working on earlier, but this meeting I cannot."

"It conveniently slipped your mind, right?" She twisted her face.

"Baby, I got so much on my plate that it *did*. If it weren't for this notice," he raised his phone in the air, showing the memo, "I would have missed it."

"I convinced myself the first year you would put brakes on this, but year two has shown me you are out of control. You're never gonna slow down?"

"Samiyah, listen," he appealed. "I can see why you're mad," he stood in front of her. "It pisses me off not being able to spend time with you, but if I slow up, I will be irrelevant in this game. Then how can I give you all that you deserve?"

"If memory serves me right, you did mighty good the first few years of our relationship. Struggle or not. We were happy!"

"I don't want that kind of life no more. A man provides," he reached into his wallet. "Here, take out one of your friends, let them enjoy your company 'til I can, okay." He took her hand into his, burying the crumpled money into her palm. "I will make this up."

"That's what you always say." She tried to hand him his cash back but he refused to take it. She released the money where they stood and it fluttered to the floor. Samiyah stared at him a little while longer before she rolled her eyes and walked away.

He shook his head at the hundred dollar bill at his feet. "I'm sorry, baby. Call me."

Her heart ached too much to do anything other than shake her head with understanding and continue walking the short distance to her car. She jumped in her Infiniti G35 Coupe and drove with no particular place in mind as her thoughts swirled over her relationship.

He pushed himself to the limit to build an empire from the ground up, thus he sacrificed *present* them for *future* them. She was torn between leaving him for good or staying with him forever, but because she couldn't imagine a life without him, she remained, thus she suffered.

Samiyah turned down her music when she heard her phone ringing.

"Hello," she answered without looking at the caller I.D.

"What's up?"

"Who is this?" she asked.

"Mannnnn," he dragged out. "Get real! You don't know ya boy's voice?" Elias questioned.

"Not when you're trying to sound all sensual and shit," she laughed.

"What's good witcha?" Eli inquired.

"Nothing at the moment."

"Where you at, nah?"

"I'm actually a few minutes away from you. Why?"

"Come swing through. We'll get into something as usual."

Samiyah didn't hesitate. "That's cool. I'm on my way."

***

"So, where are we goin'?" Artricia asked, stepping out of Eli's shower.

"Where you get that idea from?" Eli scoffed, purposely not looking her way as he searched through his closet.

"I overheard you tell somebody—"

"Let me stop you in your tracks. Since you were ear hustlin' that hard, you should have heard me tell *my people* to come get *me*." He pointed at his chest for added emphasis.

"Damn, you don't have to be rude," Artricia turned her nose at him.

"Not rude, real." Eli threw a few outfits on his bed.

"I was good for a lay but not to stay, huh?" Artricia began feeling played.

"You did stay—past nine AM. I could have given you coffee and sent your ass home soon after we finished, but the gentleman I am even allowed you a complimentary shower," Eli reminded.

"Screw you, asshole," Artricia belted.

"No, I think the word is *bye*." Eli escorted her to the front door the moment she placed her feet in her sandals.

Artricia turned around and blurted, "Don't call me. Ever!"

"Had no intentions." Eli shoved his door shut as soon as Artricia was on the other side.

Samiyah pulled in front of Eli's house just in time to see a very angry girl peel off. She knocked on his door and when he opened she giggled, "Another one of your alphabet bee-otches I presume."

"She ain't shit, nah. Come on in." He made way for her entry.

Samiyah walked into his bedroom as Elias headed into the bathroom to start a shower.

"Is this bed safe to sit on?" Samiyah eyed the sheets. "On second thought, I'll sit in this chair."

Elias stuck his head out of door. "Whatever, thuggah."

Fifteen minutes later, Elias emerged from a very steamy bathroom clad in nothing but a towel wrapped around his chiseled waistline.

Samiyah did a double take from the television and back to him. She had to admit Eli was a sexy man and it was more evident seeing him naked.

He was five feet, eleven inches, with an un-tatted reddish brown complexion. He was naturally ripped and equipped with the right amounts of everything. Facially, he wore a killer smile plastered on a baby face with a set of dimples so deep you could lose a finger in them. And his big, brown eyes could mislead any woman into believing he was innocent when he really wasn't.

He had a slightly bowlegged walk that made women question how heavy the package was that he carried below. He was simply blessed with all the physical components that made him a lady magnet upon sight.

Elias flexed his pecks. "Yea, take all this shit in, ya heard me."

"You wish," she snidely replied, allowing her eyes to settle back into her sockets.

As he dressed, Samiyah thought back to the time where they almost crossed lines.

"Let this shit happen," Elias pushed her against the wall and covered her mouth.

Samiyah returned the strength of his kiss, holding him around the waist as his hands firmly cupped her ass. He kissed her collar bone and her panting increased along with the wetness between her thighs. Still engaged in a heated kiss, Elias unbuttoned and unzipped her jeans. It felt too good, but she managed to back him off of her. She needed to think and she couldn't with the sweet taste of his tongue down her throat.

"This isn't right. I can't do this." She slowly wiped her lips with the back of her hand.

Elias shifted the stiffness that ached in his jeans. "I can for the both of us." He leaned forward to kiss her.

"No. 'Us' is what concerns me."

"We good," he swore.

She moved to the other side of the room. "If we go there, I will be just like every other girl you smash and dash and I don't want to ruin our friendship."

Elias dropped his head in disappointment, looking down toward his throbbing erection that threatened to burst at any moment. "This shit been building for months between us and now you want to bottle it back up?"

"Some things are best left alone. So don't try to smooth talk my panties off," she reproached. "It's what's best."

31

Coffee

Elias was in a state of disbelief. "So, to be clear, ain't shit happening?"

Samiyah shook her head no.

"At all?" he needed to clarify.

"Nope. Nada. Nothing. Comprende?" she made plain.

She looked up and Elias was fresh from head to toe. He wore a pair of Girbaud jeans, a crisp white t-shirt underneath a button down Polo shirt he wore open along with a pair of white G-Nikes. Two rocks weighted his ears and ice dripped from both his neck and wrists.

Within the years she'd been knowing him, he never looked less than a million bucks. Today was no different.

"Where to?" Samiyah stood to her feet. "It's whatever you like."

32

Chapter 4

After having spent the entire day together, Samiyah wasn't ready to end it and be alone. "You feel like going to the club tonight?"

"Why not? I'm game." He provided no hesitancy.

"We'll stop at your house so you can pick up fresh gear and then you can shower and get dressed over at my place."

"That works," he stated as he watched her fumble for her phone in her purse. "Who you 'bout to call?" Eli probed.

"Acacia," Samiyah answered Elias right as she picked up.

"Oh, hell no!" He became slightly vexed.

Samiyah shook her head and smiled, "Hey, mamacita. You want to get out tonight and hit the club with me and Eli around eleven?"

"Umm. If I go, Sleepy's coming too."

Sleepy spoke from the background, "Go where?"

Acacia dropped the phone from her ear. "The club with Yah and Eli."

"You can go. I'm tired," Sleepy responded.

"Oh, *you're coming*." She cut her eyes at him in a reprimanding way then continued her call. "Which club?"

Samiyah hesitated before answering, "Club 7140, but are you sure? Sounds like your man isn't interested in getting out?"

"Why you taking up for him?" She smacked her lips. "Let me find out." Acacia turned her vexation on Samiyah.

"Pump ya brakes, lil' girl. I was only giving you an out," Samiyah rebutted.

"We good over here and *we*," she stressed, "will be there tonight." She began fussing with Sleepy before disconnecting the call without as much as a goodbye.

"Why did you invite her crazy ass?" Elias didn't hide his derision.

"She be clicking the fuck out, but that's still my girl," Samiyah defended.

Elias waved his hand in the air to dismiss the conversation.

"Don't be like that, big head." She pushed and ruffled his thick waves playfully.

"I'm good." He snaked his head out of her reach and brushed his hair into its trained direction.

"You better be," she clowned.

After making it to Samiyah's house, she drew a hot bath.

"Elias, come here for a moment."

He walked in and saw she was submerged chest deep in bubbles. "What? I'm on the phone," he pointed to the receiver he'd dropped to his chest.

"So. I want your company, *please*," she petitioned.

"Give me a minute," he retreated out of her sight.

Minutes later, he returned and voluntarily began washing her body, no questions asked. "This feels so good." She closed her eyes, enjoying the strength of his touch as he sponged her back.

"I'm a fool with it," he bragged.

After their close encounter, Samiyah had been able to depend on Elias' vow to never violate. She could be pissy drunk, naked with her feet to Jesus and have complete comfort he wouldn't take it there, no matter how bad he may have wanted to.

Once she was out of the tub, he sat on the edge of her bed trying not to gawk at her nakedness, but with approving eyes he shouted, "Damn, Samiyah, you fine as tha fuck!" He shook his head side to side.

"Every time you see ass you get delirious," she teased.

He playfully tossed her panties at her. "I respect you. Could never play you like one of these ducks out c'here, but I'ma man and I ain't blind."

Eli stood to his feet, grabbed his belongings and went into her guest bathroom to take his shower. He had to get just as fresh as his female counterpart.

An hour later…

"I'll stand out c'here for another five minutes before I bounce inside," Elias warned.

Samiyah looked at the time. "Maybe they're not coming after all.

"Nah, they coming because she said so. Her ass too controlling to let him have his way. She taking forever because she probably dressed and redressed ya boy with her jealous ass." Then he sang out, *"That's why I don't wanna woman."*

"We not gon' wait no longer. Let's go."

Just as they were approaching the entrance, Acacia and Sleepy popped up behind them.

"Boo!" Acacia poked her index fingers in Samiyah's side. "The headliners are here. I told you we were coming."

"Here we go," Elias huffed.

"And what does that mean?" Acacia looked up at Elias with her arms folded.

"Whatever you think it mean." Elias remarked, continuing his walk inside.

"What's his problem?" Acacia asked Samiyah, pointing toward his back.

Choosing not to read her for taking so long, Samiyah simply responded, "Nothing that a good time won't cure. Let's party."

As they made their way through, the music immediately grabbed ahold of all of them. Eli two-stepped his way through. Samiyah sashayed with a sexy bounce. Sleepy bobbed his head to the beat despite his protest to be there and Acacia swayed lightly as she scouted the social scene with her delusions of competition in full effect.

35

Everyone stood in line to get their drinks at the overly crowded bar.

"Is it ladies' night?" Samiyah looked at the abundance of females gushing through the doors. "Where all the men in this piece?"

"Who really gives a shit when da man's right c'here?" Elias grinned as wide as a Cheshire cat.

Acacia cozied up to Sleepy, pumping her pelvis against his body. "Let's dance, Papi."

"Ha she gon' Merengue up a thuggah thigh off of 'Red Rum'?" Eli looked at her with disdain.

"Really though?" Samiyah acknowledged Acacia's clinginess.

Elias leaned into Samiyah. "Aye, I'ma go 'head and check out this joint." Eli pointed in the direction he was heading.

"Cool. I'll go find us a table." Samiyah scouted the massive club until she found a vacant spot.

No sooner than Samiyah sat down a gentleman approached her.

"Can I get you a drink?" An older man asked as he prepared to sit next to her.

"Does that offer come with conversation?"

"Of course," he smiled, showing his one lonely gold.

Ugh. Without hesitation she sharply replied, "Then *no.*"

He got up as smoothly as he sat down, fixing the lapel of his jacket as if what she said didn't faze him any.

Way to shake it off, playa, she thought.

She swayed to the sound of Frankie Beverly's *Before I Let Go,* while sipping her drink.

Twenty minutes later, Acacia led Sleepy closely by the hand to locate where Samiyah was. Once she found her, she plopped down next to her, completely out of breath.

"Want a drink, baby?" Sleepy asked, standing alongside her.

"Why didn't you say something before I sat down?" Acacia was about to stand up to go with him, but Sleepy gently nudged her to remain seated.

36

"I can manage getting a drink by myself," sarcasm resonated in his tone. "Refill?" He pointed at Samiyah's cup.

She shook her head *no*. "I'm straight."

Acacia's eyes followed him until he vanished into the thick of people flinging their bodies around to the music.

"I'll be right back." Acacia rose to her feet once more.

Samiyah grabbed at her arm. "Sit'cho ass down. Be easy."

"You don't get it." Acacia shook her head.

"You're right. I don't." Now it was Samiyah's turn to shake her head. "Enjoy yourself and quit looking for a reason to buck." Samiyah said above the music as Acacia turned around in her chair to see if Sleepy was on his way back.

The way Acacia obsessed over him would have led anyone to think she was hideous looking dunt-ta-dunt. But she was the exact opposite. Acacia stood five-five, small framed but curvaceous. Her olive skin tone—unblemished, her eyes—sultry, but her dynamic smile was always the eye catcher. Too beautiful on the out, to be so unpretty on the in.

Ten minutes had elapsed. "Where is he? It doesn't take *that* long." Acacia became worried, rose to her feet and refocused her attention as she searched the crowd twice more.

Ignoring her question, Samiyah giggled, "Let's dance." But before Samiyah could stand, snap a finger or sling her hair back, Acacia was gone. Samiyah had to shift through the masses and hot tail behind her with the hopes she could catch her before she made a fool of herself.

In Acacia's desperate pursuit to find Sleepy, she found more than what she was anticipating.

"What the hell? You were supposed to be bringing me a drink," she announced piercingly. "But instead you—" she twisted her neck to the woman who was standing nearby, then glared back at Sleepy, "talking to a *bitch*?"

The woman she referred to looked confused because she had no idea what was going on and why she was referring to her in that manner.

Sleepy couldn't risk Acacia going in her bun to retrieve the blade she hardly left home without, so before the woman could respond in her own defense, Sleepy quickly dragged Acacia out of the club.

"What the hell is wrong with you?" he yelled, angry at the scene she was causing inside.

"Are *you serious*?" I caught you attempting to cheat underneath my damn nose." Her voice was progressively getting louder as she replayed what she saw in her mind.

Pulling her further away from the nosy onlookers, he pressed her against a vehicle. "You need to think before you act, Ma." He dropped his head in a dissatisfied manner and then looked back up. "That was unnecessary. But you don't surprise me because you do this shit every time."

"You didn't deny you were about to cheat, though. Tell me the truth," she got in his face. "You're busted now. Just say it!" She flailed her arms.

"I didn't do shit," he roared. "This was your idea. I didn't even wanna come."

"Maybe not tonight because you didn't have the chance, but you know what they say. Once a cheater always a cheater!" She shifted her weight to one leg and propped her hand on her hip.

"That happened two years ago. When will you let that shit go?"

"Oh, like how *you* let go of your brother fucking your slut fiancé? That was five," she suspended her palm in the air, five fingers held high, "years ago and you still have yet to talk to him."

Sleepy scowled at the image of his brother and the woman he once loved together and felt instant contempt toward Acacia for hitting below the belt.

"Always a cheater, huh? If you feel like that, why *you* beg me to take your ass back?"

Her eyes began to well with tears of hurt which made him instantly feel compunction. He reached out to wipe her tears, but she slapped his hand away.

"Don't touch me!" she screamed, causing more people in the parking lot to stare. She shifted her posture and wiped the remaining tears angrily. "I *begged* you? Is that how you saw it?"

"I'm done." Sleepy finalized what would be an ongoing fight. He turned away from her and Acacia punched at his back. "Go 'head. Leave, muthafucka! Go!" She pushed him forward.

He turned around swiftly, grabbing her wrists. "Dammit, girl!" He released her, then clutched his fist before his face and curled his lips. "I'm not your fuckin' father."

Samiyah and Elias stood at bay to give them time to settle it on their own, but it didn't look like that would happen without intervention. So, they cautiously approached the quarreling couple.

Sleepy stepped to Elias. "Tell her what happened in there, man."

Elias exhaled in disgust, then chuckled softly. "Check it. Lil' mama was tryna get at me. Told her I was single. She didn't believe me, so she asked my man right here," he explained, tapping into Sleepy's chest. "And boom, that's when your melodramatic ass showed up."

Acacia still didn't believe it. Samiyah saw in her face she was preparing to refute Eli's story, but Samiyah dragged her off to the side to talk sense into her.

"You know just like I know he didn't do shit wrong. Can you swallow your pride, insecurity, or whatever the hell got into you tonight and realize you're blowing this way out the water?"

Acacia remained silent. She was too prideful to admit she was more than likely wrong, but her eyes were remorseful and that was enough for Samiyah. She walked her back over to where Sleepy stood talking to Elias. Acacia stepped in front of him silently, but with attitude still apparent.

Sleepy acknowledged the broken woman before him. He knew her tough girl act was just that. "You know I won't hurt you."

Acacia went about things the wrong way, but she only needed reassurance because Mrs. Hyde left her body just like that.

"See why I don't really fool with her? She throwed the fuck off," Elias said to Samiyah as he observed the change in her demeanor.

"She got her issues but she good peoples, for real," Samiyah spoke up for her although she too believed Acacia was too neurotic concerning Sleepy.

"We're about to go home," Acacia said, standing in Sleepy's embrace.

"You good. I'm ready to go, too. It's three thirty in the morning and I am over this night," Samiyah yawned and then looked to Eli. "You ready?"

"Go home," Eli suggested, shooing Samiyah away.

"You rode with me, though."

"The girl I was hollerin' at will give me a boost." He smiled mischievously, tilting his head toward the club.

"Just nasty," she teased. Watch your ding-a-ling fall off from over-usage." Samiyah grabbed at her crotch area for demonstration.

"Funny—*ha ha* funny, but we," he pointed at his soulja, "will keep rollin' like an eighteen wheeler."

"If you sure, then I'm out." She headed to her car that was parked nearby.

He chunked the deuces and headed indoors. The honey whose name he didn't know was patiently waiting for his return.

Chapter 5
Elias...

"**G**ood morning," Sunsa'raye sang into Elias' ear.

Jumping up in a mild hysteria, he stammered, "What the—" He was shocked to see the woman from last night still in his bed. He pulled the covers off of him, sat up, massaged his fingers over his throbbing temples and moaned. "Man, I thought you left."

"And why would I have done that?" She sat her half naked body upright, curious for a response.

Answering her question with a question, he replied. "Why wouldn't you have?"

She took immediate offense. "That's real fuckin' rude! A bitch gives you some ass 'cause she's 'bout it and now you wanna toss me out like trash?"

She watched him get dressed nonchalantly. "You're not trash," he said and her shoulders relaxed. "But, you are a *bitch* like *you* said," he added calmly.

"*Oh, no you didn't*!" she grimaced, taken aback. "I can see why yo ass is alone. You low down and you ain't worth shit," she spewed.

"And that's coming from a woman who upped the pussy with no hesitation."

She dressed herself as fast as she could, tripping over herself. Still suffering from her hangover, she slurred, "You ain't nothing but a dog."

"Bow wow," he chuckled. "Hope you enjoyed coming up with fleas," he teased as he closed the door behind her.

With no consideration of how he played the game raw, Elias sat down on his plush leather sofa, kicked his feet up on the coffee table and turned on his sixty inch flat screen.

He had been a womanizer as far back as he could remember.

His father, Mack, con-man extraordinaire before he died, showed Elias up to the age of twelve how to be a chauvinistic man by the examples led within his home. Carolina Red, his mother, reinforced that a woman will stand up just as many times as she'd been kicked down. His uncle, Flint, picked up where his brother, Mack, left off. He further raised Eli on a parallel yet different course. He educated him on principle, code, and honor. He taught him that pimp was inevitably in his blood and he didn't have to front about a damn thing.

Although he never engaged in the grind and glory of pimps and hos, he did however, live by many of the creeds his uncle instilled in him. One of them being—*Celebrate when a ho goes, she just made room for the next bitch!*

Acacia and Sleepy…

The smell of breakfast brought Sleepy out of their master bedroom and into the kitchen where Acacia stood over the stove with nothing but his t-shirt on.

"Good morning, Papi chulo." She looked back at him with doe eyes.

"Buenos dias, bonita." He inhaled deeply with his nostrils flaring widely to embrace the irresistible aroma. "Ummm, is that Mallorcas on the grill?"

She smiled sweetly, "Sure is. Plus we have ham, eggs, and cheese."

He rubbed his hands together as that was one of his favorite meals and Acacia knew it. They shared a brief kiss before she refocused her attention to plating her make-up meal.

"Have a seat." She pulled out a chair. She placed the dish before him and instant thoughts of home in Puerto Rico came flooding to his mind.

Acacia took a sip from her banana milk as she adoringly watched him.

"About last night," Sleepy began.

She exhaled loudly. "Papi, let's not talk about that," she whined as she rubbed his thigh. "We just made love and everything is so good between us." She slid into the space between the table and his body, straddling him, "Aren't they?" She stuck her lips out.

"Sex as a weapon?" Sleepy tilted his head as he looked at her.

"If it will get me what I want, then the answer is *yes*," she giggled.

He smacked and cupped her butt cheek. "I have to leave for work, but we *will* talk about this later." He stood to his feet, lifting Acacia with him. He kissed her lips and then let her back down.

He took his food and wrapped it to go and left out for work. She watched him get into his Ford F250 through the window at the sink and reflected on their relationship.

Together they cornered the market for couples who *make-up to break-up*.

Sleepy wasn't without fault, but Acacia was generally the reason they separated. Her mind always traveled back two years ago to an excruciating experience of Sleepy's affair. Her inability to let go of the past always complicated her present.

Sleepy had gone to his friend's bachelor party under much protest from Acacia.

What was one night out with the guys? he'd thought.

One of the dancers had her sights on him the entire night, it was hard not to. Sleepy had the sexiest, sheepish bedroom eyes on any man. They sucked you in and held you captive. Although she was inviting as hell, he resisted her up to the point where the high of him

43

Coffee

rolling and drinking kicked in. Her flirting turned into her having her sexual way.

Overwhelmed with guilt, he went home and explained to Acacia exactly what happened and with much regret, but it didn't soften her heart in the least.

"You low down, muthafucka!" she shouted as she charged him. She picked up the lamp and swung it at his head, barely missing him. She abandoned the lamp to pick up the hot iron she'd not too long ago used to press his work shirts.

She swung wildly, hitting him in several places, singeing his skin in the process. It was a struggle, but he finally managed to maneuver it out of her hands.

Sleepy's massive size alone could have stopped her in her tracks, but he tried to diffuse it without the use of force, so he didn't harm her.

"Acacia! Stop!" he beseeched.

But she couldn't hear him over her screaming. She reactively began punching, kicking, scratching, and clawing. Acacia raised such a great disturbance with all of the commotion she was stirring that their neighbors called NOPD's finest.

The police's arrival did not deter her plan to cause Sleepy the same physical pain she felt on the inside. With no response to their attempts at knocking on the door and after hearing the noises themselves, they kicked the door in. They saw both Acacia and Sleepy covered with blood and after pulling them apart they discovered that it came from him solely.

They placed a very out of breath and overheated Acacia under arrest. Sleepy, clearly being the victim, was not detained. So, he stood outside of the vehicle, watching his over reactive girlfriend sit in the back of a police car because of her lapse in judgment. He asked no charges be pressed, but his request fell on deaf ears.

The state would pick them up, regardless.

44

She spent two nights in jail on a domestic violence charge, was sentenced to mandatory anger management classes, and paid a hefty fee all because she violated a man who she felt violated her first.

She despised the fact that her forgiveness came with an expiration date. It was never her intention to drive the one man she couldn't live without away, but her past experiences that stemmed from as early as childhood kept her on edge.

He's not my father, Acacia reminded herself.

Minnie and G'Corey...

The early morning sun captured Minnie and G'Corey lying in bed in their hotel suite in Niagara Falls. She stretched her arms, looked across her shoulder and noticed G'Corey still remained asleep. She playfully began leaving kisses along the trail of his stomach, leading below. He slowly woke with a smile, extending his hands to guide Minnie toward the tip of his head, but before she could dive in, he fully awakened and jerked her upright.

"What's wrong?" She nervously looked around.

"Don't do that," he firmly stated.

She froze in place, dumbfounded by his reaction. "Don't do what? Oral? I only wanted to make you happy. What's wrong about that?"

G'Corey shook his head and smiled. "I didn't mean to startle you, but I'm good on that." He couldn't imagine Minnie and dick sucking in the same sentence. "I'll show you what I do want instead." He leaned in to kiss her passionately and instantly her uneasiness melted at the command of their intertwining tongues.

She enjoyed their make out sessions. It had to power to make her feel like she was the only girl in the world.

After a few love gazes were exchanged, Minnie draped the sheet around her naked, plus-sized body before getting out of the bed.

"One year and you still hide your body?" G'Corey pointed out.

"It's just habit," Minnie shyly responded.

"A bad one," he added. "You ain't got nothing to be ashamed of."

"You're right. It's just going to take some getting used to." With much struggle, she dropped the sheet and then hurriedly walked into bathroom.

"Want me to run you a hot shower?" she called out.

"Sure, baby," he replied, feeling like his Majesty stretched across the bed.

Minnie started the water just as her phone rang. G'Corey took the liberty to answer.

"Hey, sexy." A low voice spoke into the phone.

Looking at the caller I.D., he smiled. "What's up, Kawanna?"

"Nothing, chillin'. Is your wife around you?"

"What kind of dumb ass question is that?"

She brushed off his rudeness. "Well, I'm glad you answered. I've been craving to hear your voice. I really miss—"

G'Corey cut Kawanna off mid-sentence when Minnie reentered. "Here comes my baby now, hold on," he said coolly.

"Who's that?"

"That's umm," he snapped his fingers, "Kawanna."

She grabbed the phone elatedly. "Hello."

"Hey, friend. I know you're getting your groove on and all, but I just wanted to check on you," Kawanna lied.

"That's sweet of you. I—" clearing her throat, "we're fine."

"I heard that! It sounds like I was interrupting something. *Was I*?"

"Ms. *Nosy*, we are celebrating, helloooo."

"You're right, girl. Well, I will see you when you come home. Enjoy yourself. You deserve to."

"Thank you, girl. I will talk to you when I get back. Bye."

"Bye." Kawanna huffed as she imaged what they'd be doing once she had hung up.

"Are you ready to get wet all over again?" Minnie summoned G'Corey to the steam filled bathroom.

"If you're talkin' wet *wet*, then hell yea!"

Kawanna...

*S*hit! "Why can't I let go?" She fell back onto her bed.

Her constant desire to covet her best friend's husband would surely send her straight to hell. She kicked the sheets around from frustration and began to cry out, "*Why me?*"

Dousing herself in self-pity, she went for the one thing that would calm her. She scrolled through her phone and retrieved a picture of G'Corey's fully erect dick and recalled the particular day the photo was taken. She reached into her shorts and located her over-zealous clit.

"Oh—ummm—ohhh," she screamed as she jolted her fingers in and out of her ginger snap, fantasizing over one of the several encounters they had.

G'Corey may have been in New York with his new wife, but in Kawanna's mind he was in bed with her.

With no job to account for when she was done pleasuring herself, she curled up and went back to bed.

Samiyah...

*T*he sound of the garbage truck passing by along with her cell phone ringing woke Samiyah.

"Good morning," she chimed when she identified the caller.

"Good morning, sweetie. I was checking to see if you felt like company."

She looked at the time and saw it was 8:05AM. "I must really be on your mind, huh?"

"You stay on it. So, can I pass through der?" Cedric insisted.

The answer was a no brainer. Her heart would damn near beat out of her chest whenever she heard from him. "How long before you get here?"

"Already in my car, ya heard me. I'll be there in fifteen minutes," he estimated.

"The door will be open, just lock it behind you." Samiyah adored his attention. She always had from the very first moment they crossed paths.

They met a year ago at a reggae club. He noticed her body swaying and gyrating to the Caribbean tunes and she watched appreciation for her rhythmic moves dance in his eyes. Their sexual connection amongst many other things from then on were undeniable.

Sparks flew immediately between them and he wanted more after the first few dates. And although she admitted early on she was involved, status alone couldn't ward off their desires to have more of one another.

As time went by, Cedric didn't understand why she stayed in her relationship when it was clear Gerran was never around. The way he cared for her trumped whatever her guy displayed, but Cedric valued her too much to rush her. Besides, his father taught him, *When one man says, "Scat cat" another says, "Here kitty kitty."* So he knew it was only a matter of time before Samiyah chose him. He was too good to her for her not to.

She heard noises in her kitchen which told her he had arrived. It was shortly after the sounds of clanking dishes and cabinets closing that footsteps drew nearer and like the sweet man he was, he surprised her.

"Breakfast in bed? For moi?" She pressed her hand against her chest as she spoke in a high pitched voice.

Cedric's usually serious demeanor folded at the sight of her smile. "Fo'sho," he sat the food tray on her lap.

He'd brought her a bowl of Captain Crunch with Crunch Berries, a glass of orange juice with a slice of toast. It was real commercial, but real cute. She puckered her lips for a kiss and he obliged.

"Thank you, baby."

"Anytime, boo."

She started eating as he climbed in bed next to her. He leaned back against the headboard, grabbed the TV remote and surfed through the channels to see what was playing. Before settling on a show, he turned his head to face her.

"You know I enjoy you, right?" He mentioned as if his actions didn't display it.

"Tell me why." She sipped her juice.

He took his time to clearly detail what he liked most about her with the hopes she'd truly get it.

"Check this. You're funny, outgoing, and you have a very likable personality. You're conversationally engaging, intelligent, but not overbearing. I also like that you're confident and tough minded without being bitchy. Too much to say, ya heard me. So just know that ain't even scratching the surface."

"*Damn*! You make me feel so fuckin' good."

"You should feel good. All the time."

Samiyah never got tired of hearing him express himself to her. He was everything she craved. He filled empty spaces that were often left void. He was exhilarating, passionate, inviting and more importantly—available. But oddly enough he still wasn't Gerran.

The complexity of her feelings for Gerran baffled her because even she couldn't understand why she didn't call a spade a spade and accept that her relation*ship* had sailed. Instead she held onto that mysterious special something between her and Gerran that made *him* her peanut butter and *her* his jelly.

Maybe it was their lengthy history that she didn't want to just throw away. Time invested had to be the stronghold because he'd been having a malignant case of *the busies*. He was so consumed with making it and that desire of his was strong enough to make any woman leave without notice. But there she was, still holding on.

Cedric wasn't content with just being friends and the day would come when she would know it too.

But for now, he cozied next to her and enjoyed a together moment with her.

Chapter 6

Sunday morning came and with it arrived the newly wedded couple.

"We made it *Home Sweet Home.*" Minnie walked through the doors of what used to be her house solely. She turned to face G'Corey as he dropped the remaining bags at the door, never stepping inside of the house.

"What are you doing?" G'Corey asked her in a serious tone.

"Huh?" Minnie asked, confusion formed all over her face.

"Woman, if you don't get back out here!" Immediately nervous, Minnie walked back toward him. The moment she reached him, G'Corey grabbed her, pulled her outside and lifted her in his arms. "This is how my bride gets into her home," he told her as he carried her through the door.

"Aww," Minnie squealed like a kid.

Then her husband, smiling down at her, lowered her to the floor and gently kissed her lips. "Welcome home, Mrs. Daniels."

All Minnie could do was smile as G'Corey walked to the back of their two bedroom shotgun home with their belongings. Once, he verified that Minnie went back outside, he retrieved his second phone from its hiding spot in the house. He slipped the unpowered cell into his pocket, he would check his messages later.

An hour later...

G'Corey had a few runs he needed to make. He located Minnie to let her know what he planned on doing. He found her in the backyard in the shed, loading their dirty clothes into the washer.

He walked up behind her. "Baby, I'm gonna run by Tamera and check on my kids before it gets too late."

"That's fine. Let me wrap this up and grab my purse."

"I'm also goin' over by my mama and 'nem."

"Aww, baby, you can't go by Mama Dee another time?" She pleaded in an effort to still accompany him.

"Baby, I promised them that once I came back, I'd see them."

Minnie stopped visiting his mother's home because each time she had, Tracie, G'Corey's crazy stalker, would mysteriously pop up. Although G'Corey and his mother explained she suffered from mental illness, her sporadic ways were offensive and made Minnie feel most uncomfortable. Plus, his older sister, Renee, wasn't the friendliest person to be around either.

"It's okay then," her voice dropped an octave.

"Baby, you look as if I am going away to war. I'll be back."

With no further reluctance Minnie agreed. "Kiss the children and tell everyone I said *hello*."

"That's my girl." He kissed her on the cheek as he snatched his keys. Before he exited, he turned back toward his wife. "You know I love you, right?"

She shot him a sincere look of appreciation. He smiled in return and walked out of the door.

***

"It's about time you made it here." Kawanna extended her arms to greet G'Corey.

He blocked her hug. "On your knees, bitch!"

Her kitty ached with urgency at his forcefulness. He pushed her head down toward his waist while standing in the open doorway of her apartment. She wasted no time as she showed him how much she had been longing for him.

***

Minnie stared into the refrigerator as she pondered what to cook for that night's dinner. She wanted it to be special because that would be the first meal she'd make as his wife. She knew that would make him happy, but she also had more in store than just his favorite dish to knock his socks off!

Elsewhere, however, G'Corey was knocking something of his own.

"Who dis pussy fo'?" G'Corey grunted as he motioned Kawanna up and down his shaft with her posted against the wall.

"You," she whispered.

"Who?" He shouted barbarically, ramming himself further inside of her.

"G'Corey!" She screamed in pleasured agony.

"You better *know* it!" He spoke full of himself.

As he felt his energies about to escape his body, he brought Kawanna down to her feet, so she could get on her knees and swallow any traces of his genes. After she greedily accepted his release, she stood back up and motioned to her living room.

Noticing that G'Corey didn't budge prompted her questions, "What's the matter? Aren't you coming?"

"I just did." He fixed his clothes.

"Seriously?" Kawanna walked back toward him.

"All games aside. I have to see my kids. I just came to see you for a minute, boo."

"*Damn!* You gotta leave this instant?" She griped.

"Yes, it's called business and I gotta handle it." G'Corey massaged her shoulders.

She leaned her head to the side and sensually kissed his hand. "I guess I understand."

"That's my girl. I'll get back with ya, boo. Don't trip."

She shut the door behind him and pounded against it with her fist in disgust. "Why can't he just be all mine? Me and him like it used to be," Kawanna cried.

G'Corey's attraction to women like Kawanna were purely ani-malistic and nothing more. They satisfied the side that allowed him to do whatever sexual acts came to his mind and in the sluttiest ways. Things he couldn't consider doing with Minnie for fear of desecrating her innocence.

***

En route to his home, G'Corey received an urgent call which detoured his plans. He pulled up to his old neighborhood in Shrews-bury, got out of his car, and knocked on Tracie's door. After he made a few unanswered knocks and she didn't answer, he started banging furiously.

"Who is it?" Tracie shouted angrily, stepping from out of the bathroom.

"Man open tha fuckin' door and see," G'Corey snapped.

Tracie immediately recognized his voice. She rushed to unlock the two deadbolts, key lock, and removed the chain. "Hey, baby," Tracie lovingly looked at him.

"Don't call me *baby!*" He eyed her down as he walked past her swiftly.

She was happy to see him, so she disregarded the cold shoulder he gave. "What's up?"

G'Corey said nothing. He walked past her and into the back room where he kept his supplies and stash. One of his biggest cus-tomers contacted Tracie and informed her that he would be coming through for a pick up and G'Corey had to separate his previous ship-ment. Tracie stood over his shoulder tapping her foot with her arms folded, still waiting on a response.

"I know you heard me ask you a question when you walked through my damn door!" she scoffed.

"I don't have time to entertain yo ass. Pop will be here in twenty minutes and I need to have that man's order together. So, if you don't mind," he spoke politely, "can you back the fuck off?" he barked aggressively.

"Well, fuck you too, thuggah!" Tracie exclaimed before leaving out of the bedroom's doorway.

G'Corey would put her in her place later. But for now, he had money to make and he wasn't about to let Tracie's childish and needy ass get in the way of that.

Fifteen minutes later, Pop arrived like clockwork. Tracie walked him in the back room where G'Corey was before she retreated up front. Every now and then she got beside herself, but she knew her position in G'Corey's game.

As soon as the men conducted business, Pop bounced and G'Corey was in tow.

"Where are you goin'?" Tracie barricaded the front door. "You can't leave 'til you break me off."

"Oh, yea." He almost forgot to pay her. He reached in his pocket and flipped off a few bills.

She twisted her lips. "I ain't talkin' 'bout that," she stood closer. "I want that Gangsta."

"I ain't fucking you. So, either take this," he waved the money in her face, "or nothing at all."

She ignored his ultimatum and wrapped her arms around his waist. He forcefully pushed her off of him and to the side, dropped the money on the floor and walked out.

Tracie lived a hard life and wasn't accustomed to too much, so what she got she held onto tightly. That's why when G'Corey showed her the attention she wasn't getting from the home she ran away from, it was easy to have her eating out of the palm of his hand.

She was a wild cannon, often reckless, but dedicated, trainable and gullible. He was her first time, her first love, her father figure. G'Corey was her everything, but to him, she was just there.

She grew so dependent of him that she caused drama in his life, obsessing over him to the point that nothing was too great to bear as long as she had him in some way.

She was loyal to him because he picked up loving her where her family dropped off. At least she reasoned he did, but in reality G'Corey actually manipulated her and her feelings for him just because he could.

***

Everything was prepared to perfection. Minnie dressed herself in the shortest nightgown she owned, which was still past her knees.

She lit candles around the house and turned down all of the lights. She had the slow mix CD in the stereo with their wedding song cued to play first. She had everything but her man. But moments later, she had him too.

He walked through their house and discovered dinner wasn't the only thing his wife had ready for him.

"You don't have to bathe me, baby." He uneasily suggested. He wasn't expecting *man treatment* and fearful that the smell of sex would jump off of him.

"Let me cater to you." She tried to remove his clothing.

He playfully moved her hands away from his zipper, "This is molestation!" he clowned. "I'm gonna hafta call my mama on you, ya heard me."

She laughed heartily. "Stop playing and let me do this."

"How 'bout this? Let me drop a deuce and once I'm done you can hook ya man up."

"Ummm, heck no!" She pinched her nose in anticipation of the funk to follow. "Matter of fact, bath yourself. I will be waiting up front."

"You sure, bae?" He called out to her as she stepped out.

"Most definitely," she reassured.

Whew! He breathed out relief.

They dined on the meal Minnie managed to keep piping hot. Then afterwards, she read a poem she'd written for him earlier.

"Can I?

Can I fulfill you beyond belief with the start of each passing day?

Can I love you in one million ways?

Can I be your first thought?

Can I rest safely inside your heart?

Can I bring you great happiness that'll make you cry?

Can I be your all of that? Or can I at least try?

Can I?"

G'Corey rose from his seat, lifted Minnie's chin and kissed her. "You're a good girl. Everything a man could ask for in a wife."

"I'm glad I can please you."

"That, you do well."

Feeling pleased with his reaction, she grabbed his hand. "Do you have room for dessert?"

He hoped she was talking about a literal treat, but he knew better. He couldn't deny her, so he proceeded to follow.

Earlier, Kawanna had drained every ounce of sexual liveliness he'd had to the point where he couldn't get an erection. He tried to focus, but still nothing.

He pulled away from their lip lock. "Baby, I have an idea."

She perked up. "What is it, baby?" She placed sensual kisses on his hand that was intertwined in hers.

"Let me give you another level of intimacy." He pulled his hand back and provided a little space between their bodies.

She looked at him incredulously while her countenance dropped. A feeling of self-conscious formed in her belly. *I shouldn't have worn this frumpy, turn-a-man off gown*, she thought.

Too fearful to ask why, she simply read the sign. Minnie exhaled her disappointment but faked a smile anyway. "I suppose cuddling is nice too."

Coffee

Chapter 7

"What's up, peoples?" Samiyah asked the moment Elias answered.

"I'm cooling? You sound like you out and about?" He heard the wind blow through the receiver.

"I just finished dropping Acacia off at work and now I'm 'bout to pass over by Gerran's for a minute. I'll be out of pocket, so you already know what that means."

"Nap time," they chorused, laughing at their inside joke.

She sighed long and deep.

He chuckled then cleared his throat. "Real talk, this ain't you, dawg. You sounding all bored and shit and you ain't even there yet. I know you love him and all, but shit got its limits, ya dig?"

"You preaching to the choir. Ain't nothing you can think to say that I haven't considered already."

"True dat. That wraps that public service announcement," he remarked. "Moving on. Will you be there all day?"

"That'll be a negatory. Why, what's up?"

"Remember I told you about this joint on Decatur named Top Notch?"

"I recall." She sat parked in front of Gerran's house which was across the canal, in New Orleans' famous Lower Ninth Ward.

"I'm taking you and you can thank me later," he spoke assuredly.

"I'm honored, but I have plans with Cedric tonight."

"Change 'em." She hesitated to speak. "Yah, trust me, you'll be glad you did. So, tell me you coming?"

After briefly contemplating on whether going out to a new club was better than being with her boo, her decision was easy.

"Another time, didn't I just say Cedric's coming by? Besides, I am not about to be on my feet all night when I can have 'em in the air."

"Yea, yea. I hear ya. But you ain't hearing me. Don't make me beg you."

Elias was always down for whatever, whenever, so she reluctantly reconsidered. "Okay. I'll roll with you, but it *better* be worth it."

"No doubt and everything's on me."

She ended their call, then simultaneously dropped her phone into her purse as she knocked on Gerran's door.

"Hey, baby, I was just thinking to call you." Gerran moved to the side to allow Samiyah in.

"We on the same page, huh?"

He shook his head *yes*. "I wasn't expecting you, but if you're hungry, order in. I hadn't had time to make groceries.

"I'm good."

"Cool." He kissed her and then went right back to the grind of things, just as he was before she showed up. Although he was happy Samiyah was around, it was still work as usual. He felt in a short matter of time, all of the things he sacrificed would reap the rewards of his over-the-top ethics.

After having spent more than two hours doing crossword puzzles, texting, and the occasional roll of the eye as he worked nonstop, Samiyah fell asleep on his futon only to awake hours later to him doing the same thing.

"Rise and shine, beautiful," he said once he heard her stirring behind him.

"How long have I been asleep?" Samiyah yawned then looked at her watch.

"A few hours, you must have been real tired."

"Actually I wasn't. I can only watch so many episodes of the Three Stooges before I'm bored outta my mind, though."

"I know, baby, and that's why I'm grateful you came." He summoned her over to where he was and sat her on his lap. He admired her beautifully slanted eyes before glancing at the freckles that

60

popped across her nose. "I know it doesn't seem like I care about your feelings, being all involved with work and shit, but *you are* most important." He bounced her on his knee like she was five years old, holding her snuggly around her waist.

She giggled at his playfulness but then became inwardly saddened without changing her facial expression. She didn't want to show her mood had dropped.

Samiyah knew his heart and he really did mean well. But she had been in emotional starvation mode with him and if his good intentions weren't going to be followed up with a plate of attention, she had to continue getting her meals elsewhere. She knew it wasn't right, but she had to eat!

"Seriously, though, I know this ain't easy. We don't get together often to do the fun stuff, but if you bear with me—"

She kissed his thin lips. "Enough. I know the rest." And she did, by heart to be exact. It was the same sincere story he told her periodically.

He dropped his head and shifted it as he too acknowledged how often he sang that tune.

"I'll let you work. That's a hot song by the way."

Gerran smiled, then she smiled, touching his face tenderly before she saw herself out of the door.

While reaching for her car keys, her phone buzzed alerting her of an incoming call.

She smirked, "Hello, heffa."

"Talking to yourself again, huh?" Minnie laughed.

"Yea—yea, what's goin' on, chick?" Samiyah sat parked in her vehicle happy to hear from her.

"Girl, nothing much, enjoying my last week of being off with G'Corey before we both return back to the real world."

"I heard that. Is he home now?" Samiyah began, backing out of Gerran's driveway.

"Uhn uhn, he left out earlier."

"You want to get out for a minute?"

"When do I ever? You know I'm an introvert," Minnie needlessly reminded.

"True dat."

Minnie began their customary girl talk. They exchanged stories until Samiyah remembered she had to call Cedric before it got any later.

"Not to cut you off, but I will have to give you more of the 4-1-1 on the 9-1-1 tomorrow. Or if I don't get too caught up, I will call back before me and Eli go out, but don't hold me to it."

"And where are y'all going?" Minnie inquired.

"To Top Notch. I've never been to this club, but he swears it's all that. So, I will check it out despite my earlier plans to be with Cedric."

"I know you have to go," Minnie acknowledged, "but maybe it's a good thing you're canceling with Cedric. I don't want you reaping any bad seeds continuing to fool around with him."

"What bad seeds? This kinda doesn't feel wrong."

"It doesn't feel wrong? Well, what if Gerran stepped out on you? How would you feel?"

"*Pissed*! Without doubt because if he could creep, he could have made time for me in the first place. So, I don't see where you going with this karma business."

Minnie couldn't possibly understand relationships considering she'd only had two before her marriage. So, counseling in that area was not her expertise, Samiyah gauged.

Minnie stopped her preaching before it began. "What do I know, right?" she spoke facetiously, then quickly moved on. "Shake it, but don't break it, girl."

Samiyah ignored the flippant response, "Fo'sho. I'll call you later, a'ight."

"Bye, girl."

Until Gerran was ready to do them, Samiyah concluded she could only do her. She looked at the time and it was nearing six o'clock, she had to break the news to Cedric and then prepare for the extravaganza Elias bragged about having.

She dialed his number and he answered almost immediately. "Hello," she charmed.

"Hey, sweetie, what's good witcha?"

"The usual."

"You gon' be ready at eight, right? We have those dinner reservations at Brennan's, plus I wanna take you to Tipitina's for some good ol' jazz."

"About that, something came up and I won't be able to keep our date." Silence fell on the other end of the line. "Are you there?"

"I am. Jus' waitin' for the rest of the joke. You kiddin', right?"

"Afraid not."

"Is it an emergency or something?"

"No. Nothing like that."

"Oh, so you blowin' me off for dat Gerran cat?"

"Not at all. It's Eli."

"Unless there's a good reason, Eli don't make it no better, ya heard me."

"He says it's one," her tone remained soft.

It made no sense for Cedric to go back and forth with her on the matter. He decided to take his L like a man and not press the subject.

"I dunno know what it is about you, but I got a sweet spot for ya. I guess I can get out with the fellas instead and we save this here fa anotha night."

"You won't regret being so understanding."

"I hope not. Get with me later."

She'd plan to do just that. It had been a couple of days since they had last spent time together and an even longer time since they made love. She was indeed ready for both.

Coffee

Chapter 8

True to his word, Eli was outside at ten on the nose, leaning on his horn ignorantly.

"This ain't the ghetto, thuggah." Samiyah cautiously stepped into his ride, careful not to expose her goods from underneath her provocatively short dress.

"Be happy I wasn't bumpin' my Juvie." He kissed her on her cheek and informed her that her outfit was killing them softly. "Uhn, how you do dat der?" He imitated Master P as he admired her looks.

But tonight Samiyah didn't need reassurance, she knew she was banging. She wore a sleek, black, backless dress that accentuated her voluptuous curves and some strappy black heels that displayed her freshly red painted toe nails.

They arrived at Top Notch in less than thirty minutes and based on the crowd of people outside, it was going to be packed indoors just like Elias said.

The club was huge, standing two stories tall and facing the river. Samiyah could hear from the outside that the inside was the place to be, even on a Monday night.

At the entry was a fine ass, well put together bouncer spot checking each individual before they were to pay at the main door.

"Do you have any weapons on your person?" he asked while he skimmed over her body with the metal detector.

"No, not unless you call what I carry underneath my dress armed and dangerous," Samiyah flirted.

"Yea, you in the right spot. Get yo sexy ass in here," he said as she brushed past his muscular build.

As she walked further into the club, Samiyah was blown away by how attractive the scenery was. She had never before seen a place so decked out. She leaned over to Elias who was feeling the vibe already.

"This is hot."

"Damn skippy. I told you this club was boomin'. And as soon as I see my girl, Cherry, I'ma really hook you up for real, *for real*," he said as he made his way to one of the many bars.

He ordered her a Cranberry and Vodka and himself a Crown. She surveyed the set and noticed the dance floor was off the chain.

"Damn," she shouted in Eli's ear, "this is really fresh." People were bouncing to Cash Money on a see through floor with translucent water flowing beneath. "I have to shake my ass on that thang." She turned around and left Eli in her dust.

Before she knew it, she had one jello shot, two additional Cranberry and Vodkas and three phone numbers all within the hour.

The deejay then changed up the pace in the place and threw a slow jam on. Taking a pause from the excitement and glancing around the club, Samiyah spotted Eli bumping pelvises with some random girl who could very well be his next hit.

Leaving him to his guilty pleasures, she perused the club. She discovered the second level of the club had a large, balcony type seating area that overlooked the bottom section.

Samiyah grabbed a seat on one of the plush sofas and looked out of the large window that ran from the ceiling top to the floor. She was mesmerized by the view of her city and the Mississippi River that flowed behind it.

Moments later she received a vibrating text from Eli summoning her to meet him at the bar below. After making her way through the wave of swaying bodies, she finally reached him and saw he was with yet another female.

"Samiyah, this is Cherry, she is the owner of this elite establishment."

Cherry reached for Samiyah's hand. "Enjoy your time here. Any friend of Eli's can most def be a friend of mine." She then pulled Eli off to the side and suggested he offer Samiyah a drink from the special list and then turned back around to face her. "Samiyah, after tonight, I trust you won't be a stranger."

Cherry flashed a devious smile and walked toward the back area of her club, an area that was guarded real tough.

Samiyah nodded her head in agreement and then excitedly nudged Elias. "Now that's one cherry I wouldn't mind tasting." Samiyah freely shared her very open opinion.

"Go for it, freak," Eli encouraged.

"Whatever! It was a *joke*. A freak I am, but a lesbian I'm not." Samiyah changed the topic. "Anyway, what special drink was she talking about?"

"Walk with me outside for a second," Eli suggested. They zig zag'd through the thick crowd until the night air embraced them. Strolling alongside the building, he looked her in her eyes. "What I'm about to say stays between us."

"Go on," she tried to speed it up.

"Say it!"

"Ugh," she held her right hand in the air. "Loose lips ain't shit."

"I love fucking with you. Check it. My peoples run a brothel behind the scene. She's a modern day Hollywood Madam."

"Are you serious?"

"Do I lie?" He wore a straight face.

"Point taken."

"Everyone knows about the club, but not everyone knows about the Champagne Rooms. But for those who do, knows that it goes down."

"How you know about it?"

"You really have to ask?" he asked facetiously. "Moving along. She has a menu of services that both women and men provide to people who got their chedda right. This the place you come to and get what you want how you want it."

"A brothel, though?"

"You say that as if it's a bad thing, ya heard me."

"Eli but it's a brot—"

"You say tomato, I say it's a thuggah's paradise. Wasn't you the one saying how bland your day was?"

"I did but—"

"No buts. This right c'here is gon' be the spice of your night."

Throwing caution to the wind, Samiyah agreed with it. "What the hell." She hunched her shoulders.

"Before you go thinking negative, let me start by saying this is a great—"

He hadn't heard a word she said. She cut him off. "Eli! I said I'm with it. Why is you still talkin'?"

"Trippin'," he answered. "Let's go," he waved her to follow. They went back inside and took a seat in a place reserved for the *Very Important Playas*.

Ambrosia, their waitress, came by their table. "And what will you two have to drink, tonight?"

Elias looked at Samiyah. "She'll have an Anaconda Red Zone with an umbrella and I'll have a Peach Head Banger raw on the rocks."

She smiled sheepishly and extended her hand for upfront payment. "I'll have your orders prepared shortly."

Eli could barely contain himself. "You know a thuggah love peaches." He pulled out his credit card and handed it to her.

In the half an hour that passed while waiting for their suitors, Elias shared past experiences he'd had in the *boom boom* room and answered Samiyah's questions over one drink after the other.

Finally, Ambrosia returned and in time too. They were one jello shot away from alcohol poisoning, but nonetheless feeling pretty damn good.

Elias and Samiyah were summoned to the back. She found herself walking through the same doors Cherry disappeared into earlier, past the same men that looked mean as shit.

She sat on a plush velvet sofa in the hall as she awaited the unknown. The nervous jitters fluttered in her stomach, but there was no turning back.

Eli sat calmly with his leg crossed in the shape of a four, slouched back patiently waiting for what he knew would be a delicious time. Five minutes elapsed and then a tall, slender, pretty face greeted him and insisted seductively that he follow her.

He rose to his feet and then looked over to Samiyah. "Let's meet at the bar once we're done here."

Samiyah nodded *yes*. Now alone with her thoughts on whether or not paid pleasure was a good idea, she crossed her legs and then undid them, fidgeting in place.

Quit being scary and calm down, she coached herself.

Now that she was a little more settled, she began twirling her golden brown locs as she gave mental thumbs up or thumbs down to the individuals who passed her by. *Yep—yep—nope—maybe,* she rated the men who casually walked past her and into their rooms.

The hallways settled and she was alone again. Fifteen minutes of just sitting forced her to find entertainment of some kind. She fished into her clutch and ending up spilling the contents. *Oh, boy!* She grunted as she attempted to squat down to retrieve her items.

"Let me help you with that."

Samiyah looked up as she heard the heavy ninth ward accent ring in her ear. He placed his hand on her elbow, gently guiding her up and back down to her seat while he himself reached under the chaise chair to get her things.

No one is supposed to be this fine! She examined his muscular frame.

"Here you go." He handed her *her* belonging, but she didn't reach for them. She was too swept up in his dreamy eyes. He chuckled, then stood to his feet, holding the towel that draped from his waist line. He eyed her down. "Sorry to have you waiting. I just hopped outta the shower. You didn't mind, did cha?"

She was stunned to a hush. He looked that divine.

He chuckled at her mesmerized facial expression.

The heat that emanated from between her thighs and underneath her dress at that moment could have warmed a New York winter's night.

He knew the play. He'd seen her type of lust many nights. So, he abandoned conversation and lifted her straight into the air as high as he could, kissing the far end of her stomach and softly biting his way up until he reached her breasts. Wrapping her legs around his waist, he walked her into his pleasure room.

The boudoir was painted a sensual red color with vintage artwork from the nineteenth century, still capturing a modern flare. TLC's *Red Light Special* was playing softly in the background. The scene was hot and so was she.

"I'm Anaconda." He finally introduced himself as he stood her on her feet and removed her dress. "And *you* look tasty."

Samiyah remained silent with the exception of her moans while his eyes and hands roamed over her body.

"Cat got'cha tongue, huh? A'ight that cool. I'm 'bout to get it too."

Anaconda abruptly pulled her in close to him and forced his tongue into her mouth, kissing her feverishly. Their oral tango told her instantly feeling like he could do no sexual wrong. She stood wrapped in his arms, engaged in a kiss wearing only her black thong. He then knelt down, pulling those off with his teeth leaving her fully naked.

He laid her on her stomach as he caressed her ass, guiding his fingers along her lower lickable lips. He pressed his body against hers, then he slid his arm beneath her stomach and hoisted her ass into the air as he plunged into her sweetness. The pressure from his large candy licker slipped in and out, stimulating parts of her that not even her seasoned veterans accomplished.

He French kissed the hell out of her pearl and she couldn't do anything but give into the explosion brewing within as she vocalized a shrilling sound, secreting a delightful cream that gave him a slippery haven to explore.

Anaconda knew there was more her body could offer up, so he didn't just stop there. He wanted to make her squirt. He turned her over onto her back, relaxed her with his soothing voice and the stroke of his hands as he continued to dine.

Her clitoris was sensitive and at his immediate touch, she tried to escape the unbearable torture that stirred as a result of his constant toying. However, when she realized she couldn't shake his suction grip that held her pussy hostage, she succumbed to his will. Minutes more and her body vibrated, her moans increased in volume, and her fingers got entangled in her own damn hair.

"*Ooooh!*" She cried as she produced water works that she'd never experienced before.

She was weak, but not done. She was primed and he knew it.

He closed his eyes, inhaled the scent of lust that filled the room as he stroked his hardened flesh. "How do you want it?"

She zeroed in on his snake as he rolled a condom onto it and she saw why he was named Anaconda. It was the thickest nine inches of greatness she had ever beheld. One eye, blood flow and a heartbeat, it was a tiny human by itself.

"Surprise me." Samiyah at last spoke, breathing heavily.

He crawled onto the bed and kissed the nape of her neck. She wrapped her arms around him and anticipated what was to come next.

Meanwhile across the hall...

"Hey, baby." Peaches blew a kiss to her favorite returning customer.

Eli was stretched out, grooving to the sound of 112's *Peaches and Cream*. "What up?" He reached out for his glass of Crown and the X pill.

71

Coffee

"I'm here to please you, so you tell me?" She swayed seductively to the sounds that echoed in the room.

"I want lip service."

"Say no more." She girdled his pants around his feet and held his trooper in her grasp until he suddenly saluted at her firm yet delicate touch. "He's happy to see me," she cooed, kissing around the head of his soulja.

"Ooh, shit! Make him happier, ya dig me?"

As the words escaped his lips, she latched on to his shaft, inhaling every inch into her dome like a black hole. She worked her mouth like a muscle, contracting then relaxing nonstop, sending Eli in a state of mini convulsions.

Fifteen minutes of her head game was enough to have him lose his cool. The way she tightened her throat around his dick sent him through the roof.

"You ready for dis vitamin D shot?" He felt his heated liquid rising to its opening.

Peaches said nothing, but began sucking even faster, latching on tighter. He growled. She winked. He came.

Back on the other side of wonderland...

Samiyah showered then redressed panty-less. Anaconda sat on the corner of the bed naked still and watched her walk toward the door. She turned around to wave bye and he made his dick jump a few times as if to say bye back, then grinned. She couldn't help but laugh before she exited room.

She headed back through the double doors and into the club. P-n-C's *Let the Good Times Roll* was playing and it was the perfect jam to sway to the bar where Elias was scoping the sexual scene.

Samiyah wrapped her arms around his waist. "That was one hellava drink!" She broadcasted before taking a seat next to him, hands still on Eli's person.

72

"I'm still feinding, yea." He held up his hand for her to stop. "Don't touch me." Elias shivered at her touch then literally shook his entire body to shake the lust off.

He caught the bartender's attention so he could send drinks to the ladies nearby. He had more go-go juice to release and those two chocolate bunnies sitting at the end of the bar would more than likely satiate his urges.

He swiveled toward Samiyah who was dancing in her chair, anxious to tell him of the time she had when he saw trouble approaching. "Heads up." He nodded to get her to look over her shoulder.

No sooner than she did, she was confronted.

"What's good?" He looked squarely at her, then at Elias and then back to her. "Samiyah? You eighty-sixed me to do this right c'here?" The delivery of Cedric's questions were cold.

Standing up, she placed her hand on his forearm. He backed up slightly which made her tilt her head. Maybe the shift would help her recognize who she was looking at.

"Let's go somewhere private and talk. I don't do laundry outside."

"No need, bruh," he said nonchalantly.

"Bruh? Since when we rock like that?"

"Since tonight. Look, don't act like you care what I think, nah. You played me when you knew what was up with us tonight—and fa dis?" He looked around confused. "Go 'head, finish doin' you."

"Wait a minute. You gettin' besides yourself now. Let's talk someplace else," she spoke between pursed lips.

Elias kept his back turned to give them space, but if their lover's quarrel escalated to anything remotely disrespectful, he would have to intervene.

"I see ya boy, Gerran, taught you well. Mannnn, I'm out!"

That was a gut busting statement because she knew she was nothing like her boyfriend in those regards and her heart broke to see him angrily walk away. Matter of fact, she *was* him each time

Gerran canceled on her, so she knew the look and sound of disappointment when she saw and heard it.

Unexpectedly running into her, and there of all places, showed him that all he did accounted for nothing. He not only played backseat to Gerran, but now clubbing with Elias too?

She wasn't trying to hurt him. She had no idea he would *be hanging with the fellas* in the same spot she was, but there was nothing she could do about it now. It was done. He was gone.

"You a'ight?" Elias questioned.

She turned around to face him. Her high was over and it showed. She leaned into the curve of his arm. "Just take me home, please," was all she said.

Chapter 9

"**L**ook who decided to answer?" Tamera huffed into the phone.

G'Corey glanced at the digital clock that read 6:15AM then over to Minnie to double check that she was asleep still. "What's up?" he sluggishly replied.

"What's up?" she repeated dubiously. "What's up is how you left *your* kids hanging the other day. You told them you were coming over, but of course you didn't. I swear yo ass makes me sick. But the next time you make them a promise, thuggah, you better keep it."

"Is that why you called? To go off?"

"Yes and no. I actually need you to bring your children to summer camp this morning, but reading you was a bonus."

G'Corey breathed a sigh of uncertainty as if he really had a choice in the matter. He loved his kids, he just didn't appreciate how Tamera made it seem as if the world would come to a screeching halt if he didn't do every single thing he said.

With sleep still upon him he begrudgingly bellowed, "I'll be there."

"Didn't sound too convincing but I'll tell you what," she dragged out slowly, "if you don't show up this time, I will blow all your stank shit out the water to your wife. I'm tired of playing with you when it concerns them. You got twenty minutes!" She terminated the call on that note.

G'Corey was pissed, but he couldn't afford for Tamera to call back and put Minnie on any bullshit alert. Tamera was a compelling story teller and she knew above all people how he rocked. So, there was need to call her bluff.

He rolled out of bed, but not before tapping Minnie to let her know he would be leaving out. But she was out cold, so he just got dressed and left.

On his drive over, he reflected on the day that changed everything between him and Tamera.

"Tamera, do you not care? Or are you just that fuckin' stupid?" Tracie stopped Tamera in G'Corey's driveway before she could start her engine.

"What did you say?" Tamera asked, stepping out of her car and walking up on Tracie with her protruding belly arriving first.

"I tried to let you fade to black like the rest of those bitches he fuck around with but you just won't go. Now you done trapped him into proposing to your ass because of your pregnancy." She flicked her finger up and down at her stomach, wearing a stank face.

Tamera gave her the brick wall. "What the hell eva, Tracie. You will say anything to get a rise out of me, but listen to me carefully." She stood close enough to kiss her. "G'Corey is my man, not yours! You can fantasize all you want, but that's all it will ever be."

"You can believe whatever stories he tells you about me being crazy if you like. But I can tell you a very different and intimate story about us."

"I'm done." Tamera turned around to leave.

Tracie blurted out behind her back. "G'Corey has a four inch birth mark that can be seen once all of his pubic hairs are shaven." Tamera froze in place with her back to Tracie still. "That got your attention, huh?" She laughed. "He laughs a little when you suck his crooked dark dick after he cums because it's ticklish. Well, I don't know if you can please him as I can, but in case you didn't know— yea, that's his sensitive spot."

Tamera's blood was boiling. She turned back to face Tracie. "Don't stop. Tell me more about how you're evidently fucking him."

"You are stupid," she giggled. "He hates condoms and he loves—"

Whop! Tamera socked Tracie with a stiff left hook. The engagement ring she wore tore into Tracie's jaw and drew blood immediately. Tracie laughed even harder as she spit blood from her busted mouth onto the pavement.

G'Corey ran in lightning speed from down the street when he was able to identify the two women getting into a brawl on his block. Tracie leaned back and pulled her fist back, she was about to deliver the ass whooping she been desperately itching to give Tamera.

G'Corey caught her arm in mid attack, damn near breaking it as he twisted it behind her back. Then he kicked her in the ass so hard it forced her into the street and she fell on her behind.

"Are you alright?" he asked Tamera. She looked at him with contempt and slapped the crap out of him. Huffing and close to tears, she twisted the ring off of her finger and threw it at him.

"I've had my suspicions, but now I know. We are over! So, don't try calling me. I'll let your mother know when I have the twins!" she screamed at him before turning and stalking off to her vehicle. G'Corey ran up behind her and grabbed her arm, preventing her from closing the door. "Let me go!" she screamed.

"No! What happened? Come inside," he tried to convincing her to talk.

"Stop!" she barked, but G'Corey refused as he tried to get her out of the car. She fumbled through her purse with her free hand, found her mace and sprayed him.

"Aaahhhh! Shit!" He began coughing and backing up, trying to fan the burn in his eyes and prevent an asthma flare. He stumbled, leaning against the porch of his house. Tamera slammed the car door and screeched off.

Tracie watched everything unfold and loved every second of it. Finally, it would be just the two of them again. She ran over to him.

"Are you okay?" She questioned him over his groaning. "You're alright?" she asked again.

Once she was close enough to touch, G'Corey grabbed her by her shirt and rammed her against the house. He bit his lip almost breaking skin as he slammed a devastating blow to Tracie's face, shattering her jaw on impact.

She crumpled to the ground, knocked out cold.

"Aaahhhh," G'Corey released his pain into the sky. Tamera was the best person he'd ever met and he knew there was no way of winning her back. So whatever was said to disrupt his life with her was worthy of beating the shit out of Tracie. He walked away, but when he looked over his shoulder and saw her lying there, it angered him once again.

He rushed up on her, lifted his foot damn near toward his chest and allowed it to come crashing down on her pelvis.

He hocked phlegm from his pit and spat on her broken body.

Tracie mentally blocked out that attack as she'd done all others, but her body's constant reminder of that day was the limp she still has in her walk and the offset of her bite.

***

The thud at the door woke Minnie out of her sleep. She looked over for G'Corey to answer, but then vaguely remembered he had left some time ago.

Minnie mustered the strength to swing her feet outside of the bed and into her fuzzy house slippers. Then she willed herself through the house, opening the front door with half opened eyes.

"Good morning, sleeping beauty. Didn't mean to disturb ya. I only wanted to drop this off before more time passed." Yuriah said, holding her belated wedding gift.

Minnie and Yuriah grew up in the same neighborhood, went to the same church, and ultimately became childhood friends that had maintained a bond well into adulthood.

After ushering him inside, she disappeared to change out of her pajama pants and shirt as well as conduct her hygiene regiment before returning. This time she greeted him with more enthusiasm. "Good morning, Yuri," she hugged him.

He patted the medium sized box next to him. "You didn't have to get all dressed, ya heard me. I was just bringing you ya present."

"I needed to get dressed, so you're good. But do you mind telling me why didn't you come to the wedding, mister? I looked for you and even called you twice, but you never answered." Minnie placed her hand on her hip in a *Big Mama* kind of fashion, waiting on his explanation.

"I couldn't get out of bed that day. I was sick as a dog."

"Awwww. I didn't know that. And here I was, about to jump down your throat. I'm sorry."

"It's all good."

"No, it's not. I could have asked without the attitude." She shook her head reproachfully. "How about I make it up with better manners? Stay for breakfast, please."

Yuriah only had intentions of dropping off the gift and leaving. He wasn't fond of the choice she made in a husband and it was better if they remained separate of one another's company. "No harm. No foul. I'm promise you I'm good, so I'm 'bout to be out."

"Please, I rarely see you these days." Minnie petitioned once more.

She looked up at Yuriah with the same doe eyes that always softened his heart for her.

He did miss her. She'd been his only female friend since he could remember. "A'ight, if you insist."

"I do insist, so follow me." She led the way through her shotgun home and into her kitchen, pulling out a seat for him to take at the table.

"I'll make some cheese grits, eggs, and sausage. How does that sound?"

"You know I don't—" Yuriah was cut off in mid-sentence.

"Eat pork? Yes, I know. I have turkey sausage. You don't think I know you like I know myself?"

Yuriah didn't answer, he just gave a simple head nod to show his agreeance.

They went back and forth, laughing to the point of tears at old stories and reliving memories from back in the day that for a moment Yuri almost forgot things had changed drastically between them.

A short while later, that drastic change arrived to a delightful smell that almost made his eyes roll backwards.

"Bay-bae, you tearin' it down in der." He spoke loud enough for her to hear as he walked toward the aroma. Once he made it to her, his smile dropped. He saw an unwelcoming look on Yuriah's face. He addressed him anyway. "What up? What brings you to my neck of the woods?"

Yuriah said nothing.

Minnie sensed a bit of disharmony between them and spoke for him. "He brought us a wedding present, but now he's our breakfast guest. And you my love are just in time. Have a seat." She pulled out her husband's chair.

G'Corey watched his wife serve him first and then Yuri before she plated her food last and took a seat. "As our guest, do you mind saying grace, Yuriah?"

"A'ight," he agreed. They all bowed and closed their eyes as he uttered the blessing.

When he was done they each chorused, "Amen."

"Thank you, Yuri. That was nice," Minnie complimented.

"Humph. Since when do sinners have souls?" G'Corey threw salt on him. He never liked how Minnie saw no wrong in Yuriah, but if only she knew her saint was an angel of death back in his street day.

"You ever known me to fuc—" He cleared his throat, "play around withchu?"

"Who's playing? You *know* what I meant?"

Yuriah knew exactly what he intended. G'Corey was referring to the devastation he and his goons reeked when they had the dope game in a choke hold. Yuri and his people ruled the streets of uptown New Orleans with an iron fist.

Munch, Kamal and Yuriah were brothers as well as three lines you did not want to cross—ever.

The hoods made them legendary because they did as young men what some died never having accomplished. Over the years, they managed to turn drug dollars into a fortune unheard of. They washed their millions through different investments, real estate and more. But the price of it all cost a lot of men their lives on both sides and there was nothing glorious about laying a man down.

"I don't." Minnie sat confused, looking innocently between both men.

"Nothing to brag on. Knuckle head stuff. That's all," Yuriah assured Minnie. Glaring back at G'Corey, he shook his head. "And for what you think you know, trust me you know zilch. So, insinuate nothing about me, ya heard me." He locked eyes with him to solidify his seriousness.

"Is everything alright with y'all? Minnie didn't like the tension between them.

"It's all good, baby. Just a little bit of man talk, that's all." G'Corey reasoned.

"Well, let eat before it gets cold, okay?" Minnie raised her fork to her lips.

Neither man spoke, but they both began eating at her request. The silence during the meal rose major concern for her because it was her hope that her best friend and husband could grow to like each other someday. But each time they were in the same room, that day of friendship seemed to be further away.

Moments later, Yuri pushed away from his plate. Wiping his mouth with the nearby napkin, he thanked Minnie for breakfast. "This was good, but I gotsta be goin' now."

"I'm so glad you stopped by and although this goes without saying, but you're welcome here anytime." Minnie reminded him not to be a stranger.

"I feel you." Yuri smiled her way before standing to his feet to leave.

"G'Corey." Yuriah firmly called out.

"Yuriah." G'Corey slouched in his seat and spoke nonchalantly.

"Why so formal, you guys? We're family," she reminded them.

Minnie tried so hard to have her friends accept her spouse. At times it seemed like a struggle, but they would have to eventually because G'Corey was there to stay.

***

"What time is it?" Eli asked with one eye opened, yawning and scratching his manly trail.

"It's almost noon," Samiyah replied.

He looked down and smiled at his mid-day erection, then leaped out of her bed and headed to the guest bathroom down the hall to shower. He was seconds away from stepping under the rush of hot water when he realized he needed Samiyah to run get his things. He peeked out of the door and called her name until she responded.

"What?" She yelled back to him.

"Can you get my *You Never Know If You Got a Double Stacker and You Might Need to Get Fresh* bag out of my truck?" He stated in one breath.

She stopped at the door. "Boy, you stoopid. Where are your keys?"

"They're in my jeans on the floor next to your bed."

She headed back to her bedroom. As Samiyah went through his pockets, she saw the receipt for last night's grand slam. *Holy shit!*

Club admission $30, drinks for the night $80, an Anaconda Red Zone $700. To be sexed like there's no tomorrow – priceless!

Samiyah put his ticket back where she found it. She retrieved the keys to his Escalade and did as he asked.

The moment she opened her door the mid July heat began scorching her skin. She zipped down the steps from her second floor apartment and caught the eye of her old as Methuselah neighbor shining the rims of his ride.

"How are you today, My-Mya?" He leaned against his car.

"It's *Sa*miyah and I'm fine, Mr. Johnson." She reached into the backseat of Eli's vehicle, trying to ignore him but she could still feel his old, perverted eyes staring.

"I see you fine, I asked how are you? And how many times do I need to tell you to call me Eddie?"

"I am good. And I will always call you Mr. Johnson.

"Wait a minute, Samiyah. When you gon' let me take you out to dinner? I'll be on my best behavior. I promise."

"No offense, but your flirting is repulsive."

"You say that now because you not used to a refined man, but you'll come around one day. Just hope I still want you." Mr. Johnson resumed polishing his car.

By the time Samiyah made it inside, Elias was stepping out of the shower. She handed him his bag and took a seat on the counter.

"Last night was wild I only wish it didn't end the way it had."

"Man, Cedric acted like he was your main thuggah. He knew his role and if he forgot, last night refreshed that ass."

"It's not like that. I dissed him for something I could have done with you any night except last night."

"Don't go beatin' yo'self up. He got two choices from this point. "Deal or no deal," Elias spoke straight forward.

"Not everything is cut and dry, you know?"

"Sure it is, when you don't give a damn either way. I see things like this, either it is or it isn't. She will or she won't. You're in or you're out. See where I'm goin' with the either or's? Don't complicate shit with all the extras. Take it for what it's worth and move the hell on from there."

"You always give such sensitive advice," she spoke facetiously as she slapped him on the back of the head.

"I do my best."

"Changing subjects, how often do you play the back rooms over at Top Notch?"

"I go whenever I get the urge, maybe twice a month."

"Damn, balla! Help me understand something. All the ass you get for free, why spend for it?"

"Easy explanation. Free comes with drama. W*hy I gotta go? You wrong for that! Why can't I meet your people?*" He mocked in a female's whiny voice. "But money indicates business. I want it, you got it. So like Soulja Slim, I'll pay for it, if I want it."

"I heard that. Well, what's on your agenda today?" Samiyah watched Elias once over his appearance.

"Later on, me and Jacobi goin' to a party, uptown. Why, you wanna roll?"

"Nah, I'm gonna see about making amends with Cedric."

Elias brushed his waves and checked himself again. He couldn't hit the set without being on point.

"You look damn good," Samiyah commented.

"I know it. At least that's what the mirror told me." He turned around and kissed Samiyah goodbye. "I'll holla lil' mama."

Samiyah saw Elias out of the door, then almost immediately picked up her phone after his departure.

Usually Cedric would have called her, but it was clear he was upset still. She called him, but he didn't answer. She redialed his number, but it was the same nothing result. So she left a message with the hopes he'd call her back once he heard sincerest apologies.

She knew Elias' take on the matter and if she talked to her friends, Minnie would ultimately ease Gerran into the conversation and Acacia would somehow make it about her man. So, the only person she thought to call was her *day one* friend.

"Mama, you busy?" she asked the moment her mother answered.

"Not for my baby. What's on your mind?" Her mother detected anxiety in her voice.

"It's about Cedric."

Ms. Mary listened without judgment and once Samiyah finished crying over spilled milk, her mother spoke.

"No one wins when you love with no boundaries, baby. You can't have him and *him* on *your* terms. Someone, if not everyone, will be hurt. If you love Gerran, which I know you do, then get it together. But if you choose Cedric, sever your ties to Gerran and give Cedric your all. Either way you can't straddle the fence."

"It's not that easy, but you are right."

Mother and daughter both expressed their love to each other before they disconnected the line.

Samiyah thought about Cedric heavily before deciding that she needed to call once more. She hoped he answered but like before he didn't.

She felt a sting in her chest, but it was clear what was understood didn't need explaining.

Que sera, sera. Samiyah climbed back into bed and forced herself to go back to sleep. It would be much easier dealing with his cold shoulder that way.

Hours later...

The constant ringing of Samiyah's phone woke her out of her sleep. She groggily answered her line. "Ummm hmmm."

"Ummm hmmm to you too," Gerran had laughter in his voice. "Sounds like you were sleep, but I need you to wake up. I have something planned for you tonight."

"Tonight?"

"Yea, tonight."

Coffee

She looked at the clock. It was 2:23PM. "What time?"

"Six. Be ready for six, a'ight?"

"Okay." Samiyah hung up the phone curious as to what was up his sleeve. Spending time with him was a welcomed surprise, but it was still nonetheless a surprise.

Samiyah laid back down, she would get up in a couple more hours and prep for whatever Gerran suddenly had an interest to do.

More than four hours later…

It was a quarter to seven when Samiyah met him downstairs. He brought with him a bouquet of exquisite roses that he held in front of his face, blocking his view of the disapproval in her eyes.

He pushed the sweet smelling flowers toward Samiyah. "Saying I love you means never having to say I'm sorry."

That lame line he got from his grandfather broke the tension before it had a chance to bubble into something. Aside from that, he was looking to fine to argue with, so she elected not to have the repeated dialogue of *why you're so late* and just whiffed her arrangements and smile.

He then headed over to open the passenger door of his Impala so she could take her seat.

Once he was inside, he leaned over to place a blindfold over her eyes.

"Wait a minute. What are you doing?" She moved away from his advances.

"You'll know once when we get there."

Twenty minutes later…

She heard him open and close his car door. Then one minute that felt like an hour elapsed and put her on edge in the best way. She could barely contain herself. "Come on. I'm ready."

Minutes later, her door opened and she felt him reach for hand, guiding her out of the vehicle. "Watch your step."

86

He positioned her in front of him and then he removed her covering.

"Oh, my God!" She held one hand over her chest with the other covering her mouth as she took deep breaths to regulate her breathing.

"This is why I was late." Gerran smiled from ear to ear as he watched her in awe over his reveal.

"It finally happened." She turned to face him. She was amazed, she stood in front of *Raw Musik Entertainment,* the studio Gerran had finally succeeded in purchasing. "You did it!"

"No, baby, *we* did it."

"What do you mean *we?*"

"Your contribution was in every sacrifice you made, making it possible for me to dedicate my time here. So, it's most definitely an us thing, ya heard me."

He touched her face and she leaned into the cup of his hand. Liquefied by his touch, a sense of relief filled her body as she envisioned how their coupled life was about to improve. He'd been enslaved to his company and that kept them separated but now with that huge obstacle out of the way, he could get back to love. Her love.

The fly by nighters, the substitute Gerrans, hell even Cedric could all get the *bozack.* She was getting her man back. It may have been a struggle to hold on, but she saw hope for their future.

"Let's take a look inside." He led the way and guided her into the empty space with the exception of the romantic spot he had set up for them.

There was a blanket with two votive candles in the center. A woven food basket sat to the side of an assorted fruit tray. Her eyes sparkled as they fixated on the flickering flame of the tea light candles placed meticulously in the shape of a heart.

"This is beautiful."

"So are you."

It was something about the way he touched her and the way his words flew off of his lips that shifted her appetite from the vittles to the *va voom*. She now had the compelling urge to make love to him.

Samiyah slowly, methodically undressed, giving him unflinching eye contact. He watched every single move she made as he admired her body under the soft glow of the nearby candles. By this point, she had removed everything with the exception of her heels.

"Lay down," she pointed. Gerran complied with no questions asked. Then she stood above him with one foot on each side of his hips. Stimulated already, her nectar slowly began to seep down the inner curve of her thick thighs. She seductively smiled because it had been a long time since she was naturally roused by him.

She deliberately lowered herself onto him and the closer she came to inserting him inside of the softest place on earth, his eye widened with delight.

Gerran tried to grab her hips to motion her on top of him quicker, but she slapped his hands away.

"No touching," Samiyah sensually directed.

He nodded his head in agreement and fidgeted with the anticipation to connect. Body to body.

The heat of her ill nana engulfed him as she straddled his pony, positioning herself on her feet. She placed her hands on her thighs and began bouncing on the head of his dick before swallowing it whole within her walls.

"Sssss," Gerran moaned. The sounds of his toes cracking under the pleasure of her up and down shot bolts of electricity from her center and up her spine.

Samiyah continued rocking him as her arousal forced her hands up her neck and through her hair. Then they traveled to her large breasts that jumped each time she moved. Gerran had to bite his fist to prevent from man handling her.

"You're ready, baby?"

He didn't ask for what. He closed his eyes and shook his head *yes* rapidly.

Samiyah teased the tip and while going halfway down, she spun around and began riding him reverse.

"Fuck!" Gerran called out to the heavens as his upper body involuntarily bolted upward. Unable to no longer resist the urge of controlling her sexually, he gripped her firmly as he pushed his hips up to drive himself deep inside of her.

"Yesss!" She cried out, pinching her nipples as they hardened with each pump. "Yes. Goddamn. Muthafucka."

Gerran was back!

He thrust further up inside and she bucked back, causing an orgasm that nearly knocked her off of her feet.

"Oh, shit! I'm cuming," she howled, leaning back on her arms for support as she oozed her cream down his shaft.

"Hell, yea! Take all this dick." His chest began to swell when he felt her sticky coat his steel.

He sat up fully and secured her by the waist as he stood to his feet, placing Samiyah on hers. They then faced the wall and she instinctually pressed her hands against it.

He separated her ass cheeks and rubbed his dick along the trail of her gushy before he plunged back inside.

"Shit! It's gonna be a long night," he boasted.

Coffee

Chapter 10

Sunday morning arrived and Minnie didn't need the alarm that, under usual circumstances, would break her hard sleep. Because the thought that her husband would be gone for the next month had her restless and unable to sleep in the first place.

His schedule was nothing new, but she never felt closer to him than she did now, thus it hurt her more than usual for him to go.

He turned over, and with the sun beginning to make its presence known, saw that his wife was watching him sadly.

He stretched out his arms to pull her securely onto his bare chest. "What's the matter, baby?"

"I—I don't want you to go," Minnie sighed deeply.

"I have to, but how about I leave you with—"

He placed tiny kisses softly around her neck and breasts. The sensations he sent surging throughout her body was explosive. His hands searched her soft horizons, then he inserted two fingers inside of her as he rotated his thumb on her clit. The feeling was agonizingly pleasurable.

G'Corey loved how wet she'd get at the simplest touch. It rocked him up immediately. He carefully inserted himself inside of her.

She winced as he stretched at her opening. He searched her eyes to ensure she was okay with more. Once she acclimated to his width, she begged he'd go faster.

"I don't want to hurt you."

She wanted to say how she might like that, but she remained silent and relished in how he always made her feel loved. So she accepted his pleasured stokes that pushed inside of her long, deep and meaningfully until they both cried out in unison, soaking the sheets beneath them.

The aftermath of their love making was the same as usual. The hairs on her neck stood at attention from the slightest heat of his breath. Her eyes watered with lingering pleasure and her legs were left feeling like cooked noodles.

As they lay in sticky comfort, the alarm began buzzing.

"Uggghhh!" Minnie bellowed as she crossed over his body to turn the alarm off. The dreadful departure time flashed brightly on the time clock and her belly filled with longing for him although he hadn't left.

"Time will fly by, ya heard me?" G'Corey ran his thumb over her misty eye.

"I know it will."

Minnie remained in bed as G'Corey showered and dressed. Twenty minutes had passed and he was all set to leave. His bags were all packed from the night before and were at the front door.

He climbed onto the bed and on top of Minnie, playfully. "Gimme a kiss. And another one."

"You're so silly," she said in between kisses.

"A'ight, I gotta go now. Come lock up."

Minnie got out of the bed and bear hugged G'Corey from behind as they walked in Cyclops fashion to the front door.

"You know the drill. Be careful and watch your surroundings as you come and go. Can't have nothing happening to my love."

"I will, but you also be safe on those waters. I worry about you out there."

He shook his head *yes* and then tongued her so hard she almost felt dizzy. "I'ma always return to you." With that, he grabbed his belongings and headed out of the door.

"I love you, baby." Minnie blew kisses at him.

He caught one and held it to his chest. "I love you, too."

***

"Papi, where are you going?" Acacia asked with barely opened eyes.

"I'm going into work. They're offering overtime." Sleepy put on his work shirt.

"What for?" She sat up fully alert. "All our bills are paid, and we're not in need for nothing."

"It's work. Not a party. Damn!"

Acacia began thinking hard, trying to see why out of the blue he was going to work, so he said. "You never worked Sundays before." Her voice hinted mistrust.

"Why do you question everything?"

"Why didn't you tell me yesterday?"

"You don't answer a question with a question. And I wasn't sure yesterday?"

She squinted her eyes as if somehow she could see something hidden that she couldn't before. Then she tightened her lips, "Alright," she conceded half-heartedly.

"I'll be home around five." He bent down toward her face, but she fell back onto her pillow before his lips could touch hers. "I can't have a kiss?"

She turned sideways, her back now facing his direction, and gave no response. He hunched his shoulders dejectedly and left without it.

Acacia felt bipolar when patterns were broken. A new set of the *who's, what's, when's* and *why's* consumed her mind. She knew being a nagging bitch would guarantee he'd leave again, but she couldn't help herself. She didn't trust him like she once had and there was no way to know he wasn't being foul unless she could see for herself that he wasn't.

When she heard him pull out of the driveway, she called both of her brother's cell phones. She needed either of their help, but neither answered.

Not prepared to give up, she ended up calling the house phone and the one person she didn't want to speak to was the one to answer.

"We're you sleeping?" Acacia asked her mother, Isabel.

93

"No," she replied.

"How are you doing this—"

"What do you want, Mija?" Isabel knew the call wasn't casual. She detected the rush in her tone.

She cut straight to it. "Can you put either Carlos or Mario on the phone, please?"

"What do you want with your brothers?" Isabel curiously raised an eyebrow.

"I just want to ask them something, Mama."

"Ummmm hmmmm." Isabel paused for what seemed like forever before she called out to either of her sons to pick up the phone. Once one picked up, she had hung up.

"Whaddup?" Her seventeen year old brother, Mario, answered.

"Do you think you could ride past Sleepy's job, see if the yard is open and if his truck's parked outside?"

"I could, but why don't you just call him?"

"Strangely, he forgot his phone on the nightstand," she fibbed.

"For what, though?"

"I woke up this morning and he wasn't in bed. My assumption is he left out for work, but I need to be sure. I am becoming worried."

"Alright, give me a chance to wake up."

"No! Do it now." She pouted in a way he couldn't refuse.

"Chill. Okay. I'll go now and that's only because you're my favorite sister."

"I'm your *only* sister," she half smiled. "But thanks, little brother. Make sure you call me as soon as you get there."

"Alright." Mario hung up the phone and began getting dressed.

Isabel knocked on his door. When he opened it, she saw he was lacing up his tennis. "Where are you going, Mijo?"

"Acacia needs me to check on something."

"Is that something, Sleepy?"

"Yes, ma'am."

"Oh, my Lord. Don't get in the middle of their mess."

94

"It's not like that. I'm checking to see if he's at work because she doesn't know where he is."

"Okay, son. Don't be long, we have Mass."

"It will take me thirty minutes. I'll be back before eight," Mario promised.

A short while had passed and Acacia's phone rang. She picked up without looking at the caller ID. "What's the word?"

"This is not your brother," Isabel spoke sternly.

"Mama?"

"Do you honestly think in your heart that Sleepy is doing something other than the right thing?" And don't feed me the same lie you told your brother because I know he's not the type of man that would walk out without you knowing. Baby, at some point you have to decide whether you are going to live in the past or the present. Learn from my mistakes. But if you choose not to and decide to dwell in your hurtful memories, don't bring my boys into it. Do you hear me, Niña?"

"Yes ma'am." Acacia kept her answer positive and short. Her mother was a spit fire just like her and she didn't want to trigger what would set her off.

"Good. And while I have you on the phone, would you like me to pick you up for church today? Father O'Malley has been asking about you."

"Not today, Ma."

Isabel sighed her disappointment. "It's been too long, but it's your life. Te quiero,"

"I will one day soon and I love you, too." Acacia disconnected the call after making what she knew was an empty promise.

Acacia's mother was a widower, not because her husband died a physical death, but because to Isabel he was dead. Roberto Sr., Acacia's father, had countless affairs and even left home for one of them, leaving Isabel bitter and reckless.

Her range of unstable emotions controlled her to the point that revenge consumed her.

After years of suffering from the mental turmoil of her first love's duplicity, she moved down south to Louisiana from Staten Island, NY. She knew if she didn't put massive distance between her and his deceit, eventually she would gain opportunity to exact her deadly vengeance.

Acacia witnessed the downward spiral of those events and how they affected her mother. She had seen Isabel self-medicate just to get out of the bed all because of a man. So the birth of her father's adultery and her mother's ill reactions to it gave life to, unbeknownst to anyone, Acacia's desperation to keep a tight hold on her own lover.

Her phone rang again, it was Mario.

"What's up?"

"He's at work. Now what?"

Acacia felt instant relief. She took a deep inhale and then let out a sharp exhale. "Nothing, little brother. You can go home now. I owe you for this."

"Cool. You can get me the latest Madden for my PlayStation."

"It's yours. Thanks. You're the best."

She hung up with her brother and the screen saver of Sleepy holding her in against his chest appeared. Acacia felt foolish, but her feeling of joy trumped.

She stared at their picture before sending him a text.

7:46AM: *Forgive my silliness this morning. I love you Papi. Xoxo*

***

G'Corey made it to his destination. *Back to business*, he thought seconds before he grabbed his belongings out of the backseat of his car. As he was heading up the steps, he heard the shut of a car door and his name called right behind it.

"G'Corey." The voice boomed thunderously.

G'Corey turned around, initially shocked, but now pissed to see Yuriah standing on Tracie's street. "What the fuck?" He dropped his bags at his feet and grimaced. "Fuck you here for?"

Yuriah remained unfazed by G'Corey's attempt to pound on his chest with his disrespectful line of questioning, but only for Minnie's sake. Because in truth, G'Corey's life meant nothing to him and he'd hate to have to show him if he went too far with his nut drop.

"Your wife is family to me, but you know this already. So you should also know I'll be a muthafuck if I let you pull her into yo bullshit blend. So, you can either be a husband or a small time dope dealer, but you won't be both. Not fuckin' with her!"

"An ultimatum, thuggah?" G'Corey's hostility level increased. He knew who Drop was, but that didn't give him permission to play daddy over his life like he was his bitch.

"I've said my piece. You've been warned." Yuriah walked away casually and jumped into his blacked out Range Rover, staring at G'Corey firmly as he pulled off.

G'Corey watched on venomously until Yuriah's truck turned off of his street. He spat on the ground and looked off into nothingness as he tried to figure out how he knew to find him there. But G'Corey failed to realize Yuriah had eyes everywhere and those eyes reported anything they felt he needed to know.

"It's still back to business, muthafucka!" G'Corey said under his breath as he furiously gathered his things and headed inside.

It was now clear whether G'Corey liked it or not, he would have to make a choice from the two presented to him or create a third and deadly option to keep things unchanged.

***

Later that evening, Elias was cruising the streets with his windows down, taking in his Seventh Ward domain. It was the typical setting, people on their porches, acknowledging the passersby such as himself.

He slowed down, tapped on his horn. "Whoa," he called out to his homeboy, Herman, right before he pulled up to a corner store. His homeboy threw his hands in the air, recognizing his peoples as he kept it moving.

Little kids that abided by the street light policy were playing on the sidewalks in front of their houses. So despite the stigma associated with the hoods of New Orleans, if outsiders could see life through his eyes, they would love the home grown fell of the city as much as he did.

Leaving from out of the store, he decided to swing by his uncle's spot that wasn't too far away. He saw his money green Cadillac Coupe Deville parked at the corner of N. Galvez and Pauger and paralleled parked his truck next to it.

B.B. King's *The Thrill is Gone* could be heard as he walked toward the entrance of the lounge. His hip hop attire wasn't appropriate to patron the joint, but his last name gave him free passage.

"Dupree." Johnny Old School howled Elias' last name. "Give me some," he laid out his hand.

"My man," Elias chimed as he slid his hand smoothly across Johnny's who continued two-stepping with his lady.

Eli crossed paths with his mother's best friend. She stopped dead in her tracks, threw her hands on her wide hips and then opened her arms widely.

"You grow to be more handsome each time I see you. My goodness Mack done blessed you with his good looks." Giselle squeezed him firmly.

"That ain't all I'm blessed with." He sexually hinted.

"You're too young." She chastised although she was flattered.

"According to who?" He looked around as if he was attempting to spot someone who would object.

"To me and ya mama. Who would, by the way, kill me if she were alive to hear this conversation." She nudged her finger softly into his chest twice. "I washed your booty as a baby," she reminded.

"And I'm just tryna return the favor," he casanova'd.

She blew his flirtatiousness off, kissed him on the cheek and laughed at their encounter as she walked over to Flint.

"Look what the wind blew in." She brought Eli to his attention.

His smile stretched across his face as wide as the Mississippi River. "Long time no see, nephew. Ha you been? Ha you been?" Flint came from behind the partition of his bar to greet his baby brother's child.

"What's up, Uncle Fly?" Elias dapped him off while embracing him.

"Oh, I can't call it." He shadowed boxed him before going in for a second hug. "What brings you 'round these parts?" He pulled from his cigar.

"Layin' eyes on ya, 'bout it. You lookin' good, Unc."

Flint was in his late sixties but looked every bit of his vibrant forties. His eyes told a deep story. His very presence commanded attention, and his dashing good looks and charm still captivated the ladies. His attire was always the same. A dapper, tailored suit—only the finest threads touched his body. Gators dressed his feet, expensive jewels adorned him and he wore his short wavy hair smoothed back underneath a slick hat.

"You too, my boy." Flint fingered Elias' multiple diamond chains. "Expensive taste must run in the family. How you sitting?" Flint referred to the money Elias had gotten from his parents' life insurance policy eight years back when he had turned eighteen.

"Still sitting pretty, Unc." Elias was in no threat of going broke. His financial security was guaranteed indefinitely.

"My man." He flashed an approving smile. "But you let me know if that ever changes."

99

Coffee

Elias nodded his head up and down slowly to show his understanding. Then his attention was redirected. He looked past Flint and onto a very attractive, much older lady. "Who's that in the red skirt?"

Flint turned around, throwing his arm over the back of the chair. "Oh, that's Lola. Lola!" Flint waved her over.

She hurriedly addressed his call. "Yes, Daddy." She smiled with her eyes.

"You remember my boy? Don't you?"

She glanced at him quickly then back to Flint. "Umm hmm."

"Show ya right, doll face. Why don't cha make us two drinks, Crown no ice."

She nodded her head as a genie would and turned around. Minutes later she returned serving them two Cognacs. "Will that be all?" She tilted her head seductively to the left still giving Flint eye contact.

Flint nodded *yes*. She then slowly twirled around and walked ever so sexily away from the men. Flint watched Elias' admiring eye and almost like he was reading his mind he spoke, "That's one fine bitch, ain't she?"

Elias had to damn sure agree.

Lola was one of the last women Flint kept around when he transitioned out of the game. When he told her to pursue her life the way she chose, she begged he'd find a place in his to keep her. He thought to tell her otherwise, but he knew that whatever Lola wants, Lola gets!

Chapter 11

You just reached N.O.'s number one hot boy, ya dig. Leave ya name and what I can do to ya at the sound of the beep.

No he is not iggin' my calls, Kawanna thought.

She had been calling him nonstop and had grown increasingly pissed each second he didn't answer. Minutes later, she redialed his phone just to get his voicemail, again.

"G'Corey! You actin' funny with me? I've been calling you and I know you seen that shit. What's the deal with you? I know you gettin' these messages, I've left you boo-coo. Hit me back!"

Moments later, "For real, what's up with you, bruh? I have been calling you since yesterday. I don't know if I should be angry or concerned. Call me back. ASAP. Bye!"

Seconds after she hung up, "This is my last time calling you. Call me now!"

Ten minutes passed. "It's apparent you don't want to be bothered. That's fucked up, but it's cool. Be like that!"

Kawanna was fuming. Although her head finally accepted over time that all she'll ever be was his side piece, her heart felt differently and it overthrew her reason. She took her frustrations out by tearing up her apartment, creating a chaotic mess as she cursed the day she met him.

Kawanna then stomped off to her room, threw herself on her bed and brewed over G'Corey's no show and no answer.

After loathing for what felt like forever, her phone rang. The ringtone informed her it was Minnie. She started not to answer, but then she decided not to ignore her.

She fraudulently spoke, "Hey, girl."

"Hey! Good news. I have an opening available. My client is a blind elderly man. You still want to work, right?"

Coffee

"I don't know about all that. I don't wanna wipe no old ass," Kawanna twisted her lips.

"He's blind, not incapable. You'll make good money and besides, weren't you the one saying you needed money?"

"Well—" Kawanna hesitated.

"Well, in that case I'll stop by your place within the hour and bring you an application."

"I guess."

"See you then. Bye."

An hour later...

Knock—Knock

Minnie was as punctual as they came. She leaned over the banister, looking at the movement in the complex as she waited for Kawanna to answer.

The door creaked open seconds later. "Come on in," Kawanna waved her inside. Minnie trailed behind her stepping into what looked like an aftermath of a tornado. "Have a seat anywhere."

She placed the application on the counter and looked around at the obvious tantrum. "What's the matter with you?"

"Nothing I want to talk about." Kawanna spoke dismissively.

Minnie cleared a space on her sofa, then grabbed her friend's hand and sat her on the sofa. "You know I'm not one to pry, but you can talk to me about anything. Is it man problems?"

"Why would you think that?" Kawanna became instantly defensive.

Minnie threw her hands up. "Don't shoot. I'm only asking. Maybe I can help."

She shook her head *no* while on the verge of crying. "Not on this. And please don't insist. I just need to think things through myself and in my way."

102

Although Minnie didn't know exactly why she was becoming sad, seeing her friend cover obvious hurt was enough to make her experience sympathy pains for her.

Kawanna sniffled, attempting to fight back tears until she couldn't no longer. It angered her to love G'Corey the way she did knowing it was Minnie he chose to marry and not her. It also angered her to know her dirty little secret would destroy her friendship of several years had it ever got out.

Minnie rubbed her back in a circular motion, trying to bring about comfort as Kawanna cried into her own lap. Minnie wiped away tears of her own as she silently watched on.

Once she was all cried out, Kawanna got up to wash her face. As she was coming out of the bathroom, her phone that sat beside Minnie had rung. It was G'Corey's ringtone.

"Want me to answer and tell the caller hold on or something?" Minnie looked at the name and number, recognizing neither.

"Nah, I got it!" Kawanna quickly ran and snatched the phone from her hands.

"Hey, Delight." She turned down her phone volume as she stepped away, so Minnie couldn't hear her call.

"Quit playin', girl. What's up with yo lil' needy ass?" He joked.

"Oh, girl, nothing. Minnie is over her, but she was just leaving. Hold on real quick." Clutching the phone to her chest, she whispered, "This is Dee and she's having a moment. I'm gonna need some privacy. I'll call you later, though."

Minnie found her change in attitude odd, but she didn't wrestle with her. She figured Kawanna would tell her in her own time what was really going on with her lately. She pulled out her car keys. "Call me, for real."

Kawanna hurriedly nodded *yes* as she all but shoo'd Minnie out of the door. The moment she shut and locked the door, she placed her phone back to her ear. "Where the *hell* have you been?" She heard no response, so she pulled the phone away and noticed the screen was dark. He had already hung up. She dialed him back, but he didn't answer. Deciding not to play the same cat and mouse routine from earlier, she tossed her cell onto the love seat and plopped down agitatedly on the sofa. "I'll be a son of a bitch!"

***

"Oh, my God!" Minnie slapped her hands against the wheel of her car.

While changing the station on her radio, she hit a pot hole and immediately heard the sound every woman dreaded. She got out of her Camry ready to take care of the flat herself until she opened her trunk and discovered her spare tire also needed a spare. "Great!" She huffed in disappointment.

It was times like these she wished her husband was home, but he wasn't. So, she scrolled through her mental rolodex, thinking of who to call for help. She knew Samiyah was in Atlanta with Gerran, neither Kawanna nor Acacia had cars and her parents were working. So that left her with one other viable option.

She dialed Yuriah. He answered as usual. "Hey, Yuri, tell me you're not busy—please."

"I'm not too busy. What's wrong?"

"I *really* need your help."

He repeated himself slowly and with more concern. "What's wrong?"

"I'm stuck on the corner of Lafayette and Gretna Blvd. I have a blowout. I really need assistance and you were the only person I could call…"

"Slow up, Minnie. You don't have to explain all that to me. Give me twenty minutes, a'ight."

"Okay. And I owe you." She quickly blurted before he could disconnect the line.

"You good. Just sit tight."

Twenty minutes later...

Yuriah greeted her as he always had, a kiss on the cheek and a bear hug. He then approached her car and knelt down to examine the extent of the damage. "Where were you headin'?"

"Back to my office. I have a meeting, but it looks like I will be late. I may have to reschedule it."

"What time is it for?"

She looked at her watch. "In about fifteen minutes."

"I'll take you to your meeting and I'll have one of the fellas at the towing company get it over to my mechanic shop."

She placed a thankful hand on his bicep. "Thank you."

"Don't sweat it."

Without another word she retrieved her belongings, locked up her car and passed him her keys. And just in the nick of time she was at work.

"Thanks again. And I almost forgot. I get off at five."

"I'll be her a quarter 'til."

Later that evening...

Minnie came outside and saw Yuriah leaning against her car. Her newly detailed car with the passenger door opened.

"She's a beaut," she said, examining how good her car that she nicknamed Pearl looked. "She looks all shiny and pretty." As she took her seat inside, she inhaled. "And she smells wonderful. Thank you!"

He closed the door behind her. "It ain't no thang, for real. I had it and you needed it. So stop thanking me." He shook his head and smirked as he climbed into the driver's seat.

"You do know I would have gotten around to it myself at some point."

"Like the spare in the back?"

"Touché," Minnie laughed.

He turned onto the Westbank Expressway headed toward the I-10 E to bring Minnie back across the river where she stayed.

"So, how was your day?" he asked, turning down the volume of FM98 on the radio.

"Extremely rough. So glad it's over." She answered while she rested her head back against the headrest.

"You want to talk about it?" Yuri looked over to Minnie with his usual stern face.

"Not at all. I just want to forget it and enjoy being off."

Yuri nodded his head understandingly.

They spent the remainder of the ride reminiscing and laughing. Minnie had a way of cracking Yuriah's hard shell. He couldn't help but release the inner kid in him that never lived a full life considering how quickly he had to be the man of his house and of the streets he stomped.

"Whatever happened to us?" Minnie went solemn for a moment. "I mean you were always there, but it seemed the older we got, the less involved in each other's lives we became."

"You were into your higher education as you should have been and I dabbled off into a life you didn't need to know nothing about. I had to keep our paths separate for a reason, but that never changed the love."

"What type of life? You could have shared that with me too."

"Nah, not everything is meant to be shared. Not even between best friends. It's kinda like how girls play with dolls and boys play with guns. We don't play with each other's toys. It ain't meant. Look, I know you curious. I see your brain 'bout to bust outcha head." He reached over the console, grabbed her hand and squeezed it gently. He glanced at her tenderly before refocusing on the road. "But we always had and we always will be close—Minnie Mouse."

She snickered, tucking her chin into her chest and slapping his arm playfully. She shook her finger at him in a *talking-to* kind of way. "It's because of you no one ever calls me by my real name, you know?"

He began calling her Minnie when she was eight. It was an appropriate fit for her short stature along with her miniature voice.

Minnie reflected on the distance that danced between them in comparison to how attached they'd been in earlier years, but she digressed. Sure they didn't see each other every day and talk on the phone as much, but she couldn't recall a time he wasn't there when she called.

"Yep, I remember that. Name caught like wildfire. Matter of fact, what is your name?" He joked.

"I don't even know," she laughed.

"But real talk, I'll always be here for you and for any reason. To help you out, protect you, it's whatever."

"Oh, I know you'll protect me, alright. Remember the Carver High situation?"

"Hell yea. I couldn't have nobody playing with my mouse. That was like playing with me." Yuriah recalled the day like it just happened.

"Stop the car!" Yuriah ordered Kamal who pressed the brakes without question.

"What's up?" Munch asked from the backseat, but Yuriah didn't respond.

Instead, he hopped out of the car and jogged across Louisa St. onto Higgins Blvd. where he saw Minnie moping along. He caught up with her and instinctually knew something was wrong.

"What happened?" His eyes drew inward as he scanned her face to determine the answer himself.

She began crying profusely and wrapped her arms around his waist. He pulled her away from him and held her at bay. "What— happened?" He stiffened his tone.

"They touched me here," she choked out her words, pointing at her over developed breasts and behind, "and they called me names," she wailed hysterically.

Some children who witnessed the boys who groped and embarrassed her all rushed to inform Yuriah of what was said and done.

One girl said, "Umm hmm. They called dat girl all kinds of black bitches when she told them to leave ha alone. They said that ha ugly ass should be happy someone was tryna feel on her booty."

Yuriah had heard enough. It didn't matter that Minnie was twelve, she could have been a grown woman, no shit like that was going to happen to her. Not while he had life in his body.

"Where dey at?" His breathing became labored and fury caused him to tremble. She pointed in a timid manner. That pissed him off even more to see she was fearful to say. He grabbed her at the wrist, "Show me!" He began dragging her down the street back in the direction of the school.

When his boys, Kamal and Munch, saw Yuriah rush the opposite way of the car, they made a left at the light and followed him.

The boys were still standing in front of the store surrounded by other kids who were just hanging. "Point 'em out."

Minnie did as she was instructed. She identified the four boys who trailed behind her, taunting her to shame. Yuriah sized them up instantly. He zeroed in on the biggest one. That was going to be the first person he made an example of. He walked up on the husky teenager who was circled by his crew. Yuriah's nose flared and his eyes told the short story of how he was about to lay that boy's ass out. He cold cocked him with his vicious right hand that landed straight across his temple, causing his head to snap to the left and his body to crumple to the ground immediately.

A riot emerged as the boy's friends all rushed Yuriah. Kamal and Munch hopped out of the car they left parked in the middle of the street to shift through the mass of people that formulated around Yuriah and the three remaining fellas he began serving without

108

mercy. His boys jumped in, but there was no need. Yuriah wasn't coined 'Drop' for nothing. Even at sixteen the hood knew his hands were deadly and he could drop a thuggah in the span of a heartbeat.

When the smoke cleared and the four boys were stretched out, it went without saying that Minnie was not the one to be antagonized. That story preceded her to McDonough 35 High School as well. No one dared to tease, touch, or mock her because they knew her people as 'Drop' although in her eyes he was just 'Yuriah.'

"There's no reason we can't make it like it was. With G'Corey schedule of being home two weeks and offshore four weeks, I spend a lot of time alone." With her feelings of nostalgia weighing on her, she continued, "I really miss our friendship."

Yuriah bubbled on the inside when he thought of the lie he fed her that she believed whole-heartedly. But he kept that newly found information to himself. He was a man of his word and promised her *ain't worth shit* husband some time to get his mind right before he did it for him. He then nodded his head in agreement. Seventeen years had bridged them together, he definitely missed their relationship too. "You got that."

She smiled and then looked out of her window. Moments later, he pulled onto her street where his cousin, Munch, had sat parked waiting on him to arrive. He walked over to his people, pounded him through the lowered window and then walked her inside. Yuriah checked the house thoroughly and once he determined it was safe, he said his piece and left.

Minnie checked the time and saw she had a few minutes until her show came on. She hurriedly threw on her sweats, favorite alma mater t-shirt from Dillard University, grabbed her Blue Bell ice cream and remote. She then plopped down on her recliner as she clicked on channel four to watch Jeopardy.

Alex Trebeck asked, "Which American Poet said, *Though the great Waters sleep. That they are still the Deep. We cannot doubt…*"

109

"Who is Robert Frost?" Minnie shouted.

The contestant buzzed. "Who is Emily Dickerson?"

Alex exuberantly answered, "Yes!"

Minnie cracked up. Her answer, no matter what the question, for all the American poets was always Robert Frost. She watched the rest of her show before she decided to gas up for her 5AM early bird shift.

She slid into her tennis, snatched her keys, cell, and wallet. She locked up, got into her car, turned on the ignition and laughed out loud. "Well, I'll be."

She then reached for her cell phone and sent a text to Yuriah.

6:16PM: You took Pearl for a drink. You're truly a class act, Mr. Leblanc. Thanks for everything!

He replied.

6:19PM: Anytime.

Chapter 12
A few months later...

Elias and Jacobi were preparing for their *Throwback Balla Bash*. They were known for putting together the hottest fall parties around. Every second Saturday of October was their time to shine and anybody who was somebody reserved the date.

They arrived at Q 93's radio station to promote their shin dig with N.O.'s most recognized radio personality.

"If you know what time it is, then you know that the hippest place to be is Rhythm City this weekend. We got two stunnas in the building about to bring it to ya. Go 'head and tell 'em how it's goin' down," Wild Wayne opened up the plug.

"What up? This that fly guy, Eli."

"And ya man, Cobi."

"And we inviting all the sexy mamas, ballas, and shot callers to the hottest club uptown." Elias endorsed.

"*Rhythm City,*" they chimed into the Mic.

"Y'all know how we do and this time around ain't no different. This year to get in you must have on a throwback jersey." Jacobi announced.

"And the guy and girl who sport the coldest 'fit from top to bottom will win a cash prize of five hundred a piece." Eli announced.

"We will also have a p-poppin' contest and the girl who works it best gets a cool five hunnid." Jacobi added.

"We got DJ Money Fresh on the ones and twos with a few surprise guests coming through to light up center stage. We doin' it big this Saturday, doors open at ten and don't close 'til ya eyes do." Elias finished.

"You heard that people. Come party with Jacobi, Eli and ya boyyyyyy, Wild Wayne at Rhythm City this weekend. Be there or nowhere at all."

**

Elias left the radio station to meet up with Samiyah. He had her make a 3PM appointment with the barber at La'Bella Donna's because his regular was out of town. He was reluctant about letting someone new fool with his head, but Samiyah swore of the chick's skills with the clippers.

"I can't be looking all stupid for my party, ya heard me. You swear with your life she can give me a Steve Harvey lining?"

"I don't know about all that, but she good. Trust me," Samiyah vouched for her. "Gerran has seen her a couple of times and he always leaves out of there on point."

"I can't believe I'm trusting yo ass, but I am. Well, I'm out c'here. What's your ETA?"

"Literally a minute. We're a block away from turning onto St. Charles."

"We're?" Who exactly is a part of this *we're?*"

"Must we go through this every time?" Samiyah sighed, referring to his disdain about Acacia accompanying them to places.

"Umm, yes indeed. One day you gon' learn that I don't like that lil' broad like that.

"Tough tittie, *we're*," she stressed, "here." Samiyah hung up the phone and laughed. Elias, not so much.

Elias watched Samiyah step out of her car. *Goddamn*! he thought. She should have been arrested on the spot for the assault she put on those mid-thigh shorts. Forcing all of that ass in her pants should have been unconstitutional. And although he hated to admit it, but Acacia was just was unlawful. Her all white halter romper glorified her sinful, sexy appeal.

Elias gave Samiyah the *you know you're wrong* look for being with Acacia, but greeted her with a hug just the same.

Acacia stood behind Samiyah. "Elias," she said in a monotone voice.

"Acacia," he mimicked her tone.

After the last stunt Acacia pulled, Elias was done with her. The only thing Sleepy needed was a skirt and the letters *wo* attached to the man she didn't acknowledge him to be. Elias despised a possessive female and Acacia took that *mine* shit to the max.

"This way," Samiyah directed as she pushed the French glass doors open.

"You better be right about yo girl 'cause I have to be on my A-game." Elias reminded one more time before stepping inside and seeing two very attractive women accommodating clients.

"Welcome ladies," One of the owners recognized her regulars. "And you?" she paused, referencing Eli. "What's your name?"

"Elias." He rolled his name off of his tongue all Billy Dee like.

"Elias?" She repeated.

"He's mine," The barber called out looking at her appointment book.

Elias leaned over to Samiyah and whispered, "I sho'll can be."

Samiyah shook her head and giggled as he walked over to his barber's station, then continued reading her Sister 2 Sister magazine as she waited on the nail tech.

A few minutes passed when the fourth owner of the hair and nail salon showed up.

"What's up, girls?" La'Tasha summoned the ladies to sit in the two spa chairs she prepared for their pedicures.

"Nothing much, we're getting prepped for our friend Eli's," Samiyah pointed over at him, "get-together tomorrow."

"Oh, yes, I heard about that on the radio." La'Tasha pulled up a stool.

"Are y'all coming?" Acacia pressed the on button to the massager.

"Let me see. Ladies," she called out, "it appears the host of this weekend's reason to par—tay is in our midst and he's right under La'Ceinga's nose."

Everyone directed their attention to Eli. But he didn't notice because he was taken aback when he saw the hottest thing moving, approaching him through the reflection in the mirror before him. La'Tasha was five-two with smooth Hershey's colored skin, and a banging body. And she walked with a confidence that said she knew it all too well.

"Can my girls and I have a special invite?" La'Tasha teased the words out of her mouth.

"Fo'sho, bay-bae. You and your peoples can be my *personal* guests."

"Fa'sho," she repeated before sauntering back to the girls.

Eli was too cool to let on that he liked what he saw, but Samiyah knew she would get an earful once they stepped of out the salon.

After an hour and a half's time, everyone was done with their services.

"Thanks guys. See y'all next time." One of the owners held the door open for them to walk out of.

As soon as Samiyah's shoes touched the concrete, Eli turned to face her. "Damn, ya girl fine as fuck!"

Acacia shook her head. "How did I know you would say that?" She looked disgusted. "You are the typical dog."

"Dog?" Elias repeated as if he was offended. "I don't fuck over nare female." He made clear.

"So what you call it when you love 'em and leave 'em?" Acacia rebuffed.

"When the deed is done and they feel played afterwards, that's all on them. It's a *fuck* thing. Ain't no *love* involved. So there ain't no robbery in a fair exchange. Mannnn, on second thought, don't be questioning me. Stay in yo damn lane."

Acacia was about to respond, but Samiyah hushed her by placing a finger to her lips. She shook her head at her. "Don't."

"Ooooww. He makes me sick." Acacia expressed her dislike for him.

114

"Y'all hate each other like an old married couple."

"Neva dat! Could never marry this broad. I would have been lodged my shoe up her ass." Elias kicked his foot in the air to give example.

"I bet yo ass would never walk again," Acacia smartly remarked.

"Bring it in, Elias," Samiyah tiptoed to lay a kiss on his jaw. "I have to separate y'all two. I will call you later." She grabbed Acacia by the hand and led her to her car. It was time to leave before all hell broke loose.

***

"What's up, stranger?" Samiyah answered Minnie's call.

"I haven't been nobody's stranger," she sucked her teeth. "I called to see what's been going on. So, what's been happening?"

"What's been going on is *you* have been a stranger. Between work, Yuriah, G'Corey, home, and Yuriah some more, you don't have time for your round."

"That's not entirely true. I always have time for you."

"Ahh, maybe if I pressed for it, but you and Yuriah have been going strong over these last couple of months. But I ain't mad, so don't go defending yourself. One second," Samiyah placed Minnie on hold as she watched Acacia walk inside of her house. She tapped her horn once her friend was inside, then she pulled off. "I'm back."

The ladies talked until Minnie made it home. Samiyah expressed that Gerran fell back into his work rut and Minnie spoke of Yuriah and all of the good times they'd been having until she saw G'Corey's car parked in its usual spot.

"Sorry to cut this short, but my boo is home. Gotta go." Minnie lit up.

"Do your thing. We'll catch up later."

Minnie rushed off of the phone unsure if she even said bye.

***

"Spending last week with you was wonderful and just what I needed. To wake up with you made me feel as if I was your girl, like how things used to be." Kawanna smelled the sheets where his body once was.

"You are my girl. You're just not my wife." G'Corey deflated her bubble.

"Whatever," she brushed him off. "I know I shouldn't, but I really love you, yea. And it's hard for me not to be with you. Like when I don't hear from you, my heart aches. When you don't come through like you promised, I get aggravated."

"I hear ya, boo." G'Corey responded more out of reaction and not because he was actually paying her any real attention.

His eyes and focus were on an episode of Good Times. He laughed into the receiver at a funny scene while a very vulnerable Kawanna grimaced, assuming he took her feelings for a joke.

"What's funny?" She felt flushed with disregard.

"Nothing. Go 'head."

Kawanna regained her composure and continued spilling her heart. Then he turned down the volume to double check what sounded like keys in the front door. Without warning, he held down the power button on his phone before stashing it away.

"…how does that sound?" She paused for an answer. "Hello?" She looked at the phone realizing he was gone. "Oh, yea, and when you hang up on me—that pisses me off!"

G'Corey looked as if he had just removed his hands from the cookie jar when his wife walked inside.

She raised an eyebrow, but didn't comment. "Hey, baby, I've been missing you."

"You have no idea how good it is to be home and with you. But they say *Absence makes the heart grow fonder.*" He touched her body all over as he pecked her lips repeatedly.

She began removing his jeans. "Show me."

116

***

When Samiyah wasn't able to reach Gerran by phone she went to his store. She was certain to find him there and he was. She parked next to him and remembered standing in the same spot thinking that the building before her meant there would be more time. But it was the exact opposite. It was a brand new project that required the same time if not more.

She walked inside, saw him and went immediately off. "Whatever happened to *bear with me? I'm gonna make time for us*?" She imitated him as she stood in the doorway of the entrance with her arms folded, abruptly getting his attention.

The volume of her voice startled him. He answered her with the same dismayed energy. "It's coming," he snapped, rising up from the base boards he was painting.

"When?" She waved her hand in the air as if to shoo away a fly.

Gerran tried hard to keep in mind she was hurting and had been for a long time, but he was too stressed to rationalize anything. "Life ain't always about *fun, fun, fun*." He murdered the word like it was criminal. "It's business too."

"I can say the same, but in reverse to."

"You could, but you know I'm right. Listen, baby, I was in the middle of all this chaos." He pointed to the freshly painted walls. "I was gonna call you on a break."

"See, your *breaks* never come and I get left unattended like always. And before you explain, I see what you're doing and I know it's demanding. But damn! What about me?"

"It will pay off but you gotta be patient."

She grew tired of hearing that word. It felt more like a bargaining tool than a virtue. That set her off.

"Patient?" She repeated mockingly. "How much longer do you want my *patience* to be tried?"

"Goddammit, Samiyah! I work hard and I freely share every benefit of my labor with you. I pay for your fancy car, your two bedroom apartment, your trips out of town, food, and clothes. Hell even the money you put in the collection plate comes from me. And you want to complain because I don't call you like one of your girl-friends?"

"No. Not like my girlfriend," Samiyah corrected, "my *boy-friend*!"

Samiyah then disappeared out of his studio/store as fast as she had appeared. She sat in her car for fifteen minutes balling. Subconsciously needing him to tap on her window, take her in his arms and apologize for being a jerk, but that didn't happen. He never so much as stuck his head out of the door.

She was tired of petitioning for his time and attention just to ultimately be rejected. Tired of having her hopes built up so they could be knocked down. But more importantly, she was tired of being a single woman in a relationship. She reached for her phone and through puffy eyes she pressed star sixty-nine before dialing a number she hadn't used in very long time.

"Who dis?" The familiar voice answered.

"Please don't hang up," Samiyah sniffled. "I know we haven't talked in a minute but if it's okay, I would like to come by. I can really use a friend right now." She held her breath as susceptibility seeped out of her pores.

His heart weakened at the sound of her voice cracking, he missed her everyday she'd been gone. He even hoped she would return, however, he didn't say any of those things. All he said was, "Come on."

Samiyah started her engine and headed over to his place. She arrived at his house in no time but sat in her car for a while as she battled between logic and emotions regarding the correct move. She was hungry for affection so her heart said it was right and although her head knew that would reopen Pandora's Box, she found herself outside of her car and at his doorstep.

His door opened and his soothing voice followed. "What's the matter?"

Samiyah looked up and his pretty brown eyes and he noticed her swollen, red ones. "Cedric. I—I didn't know where else to go."

Coffee

Chapter 13

"Communication really is key." Samiyah reflected on their all night long conversation. "You cleared some things up for me but you never explained why you didn't respond to any of my calls or messages?"

"I had to shake back. No female ever had my nose open, so I had to fall off the map, ya heard me." Cedric openly admitted.

"Don't leave me again." Samiyah shook her finger at him.

"I hope I won't have to."

Samiyah had ended up staying the night. It wasn't planned, it just happened. But she was glad it did happen because she understood much more about him, them.

He laid his head on her breast as she stroked the side of his face. She began to sing sweetly. *"You give me attention..."* Cedric sat up and watched her suckable lips move. *"You're someone who understands my needs..."* He smiled as he dropped his head to kiss her exposed thigh. *"...everything I miss at home."* She sang that song by Cherrelle like she had written it herself.

Compelled by the moment, it was time to put it out there for her to know. "I love you."

Samiyah silenced the song she was singing. She knew for a long time that she loved him, but whether it was the right time to say it out loud was another thing. She gazed at him softly. Her mouth moved but no words came out. Cedric didn't expect her to say them back, he knew that would happen in her time, but for now, he would accept the act of love making as sufficient confirmation of her feelings.

Thirty-two minutes later...

"Who gave you permission to get out this bed?" Cedric looked down his eight pack at her standing at the end of his bed.

"As much as I want to, I can't stay inside all day. You know Elias' party is tonight. You wanna be my date?"

"I have to go into the office this evening, so I can't."

"Well, what time do you get off? Maybe you can come afterwards. The party will be goin' on well into the morning."

"I have a better idea. When you finished with ya peoples, you come back to me. It doesn't matter the time."

She walked over to his side and leaned down toward his face and kissed him. His hands reached out to explore her curves. Moans escaped both of their lips and Cedric began rising for the third round in twelve hours.

Samiyah pulled away from their lip lock. "We betta stop before you miss work and I miss the party."

Cedric smoothed the bottom of his lip with his thumb as he watched Samiyah's nakedness walk away slowly. "Oh yea? Well, keep your distance, then, ya heard me."

Samiyah disappeared into his master bath where she sat, relaxed in her hot bath she just ran. All she was missing was a cigarette to chase the natural high she was on even though she didn't smoke. Replaying steamy scenes of how the L went down over and over along with rethinking his confession of loving her, had her unaware the water had turned cold. She didn't get the chance to bathe, she was so caught up in the rewind of her late night and early morning. Samiyah ended up draining the water out and starting a shower. Once she was done, she put on fresh clothes from the emergency bag she brought inside that she kept in her trunk for such overnight occasions.

By the time she stepped out of the bathroom, Cedric was snoring vibrantly with his mouth hanging slightly opened. She stopped in front of him, tapped him on the shoulder while whispering his name. "Cedric. Cedric. Wake up, baby. I need you to lock up."

He stirred in the sheets and stretched his body before he reached into his nightstand drawer. He handed her the spare key to his house. "Do it ya'self."

She took it from him and stared at it skeptically, contemplatively. "Am I returning this tonight when I see you?"

"Will tonight be my last time seeing you here?" She shook her head *no*. "Then it's yours to hold onto."

"Okayyyy. Seriously now. You told me love me and now you're giving me a key. Men don't just hand women the keys to their place especially after saying that they love them." Samiyah rambled, repeating herself as she tried to make sense of the meaning. "What do I have to give you for this?"

"Huh?" Cedric questioned although he heard her. He sat up on his elbows. "A'ight. Let me in—all the way in, if there *has* to be a catch." He smiled then fell back onto the pillow.

"Maybe being caught ain't such a bad thing." Samiyah climbed back into the bed and straddled him, held his face hostage and kissed him sensually. He wrapped his arms around her and his nature rose beneath her.

"Don't start what you can't finish, ya heard me."

"I know, right." She pecked him one last time before getting up and leaving. "I will call you before I come."

"You have a key. How 'bout you *just* come."

Cedric made her feel too damn good, she almost blurted *it* out. "I lo—" She cleared her throat. "I'll lock up now." Samiyah almost slipped and told him she loved him. It felt natural and it was definitely true, but it was sure to complicate things more than they needed to be especially because Gerran was still her guy.

***

Minnie had just gotten up from a sex induced nap to discover her husband was getting dressed. "Where are you going?"

G'Corey slipped his feet into a pair of fresh Jordans. "I'm heading out to meet up with a few of the fellas. Shoot pool, grab a drink or two." He bent down to kiss her as he examined the sleep still evident in her eyes. "I knocked that ass out."

"You won that round. I'll hand it to you, but the next one is all me. Now, getting back to you leaving, how long will you be gone?"

"It's six, nah, so I'll say no later than midnight."

She felt most insecure about him leaving. She knew her husband loved her, but in the back of her mind she wondered if he would find someone prettier or for certain finer. But she had no reason to verbalize her eerie feeling because she was the one who cared about her weight, not him. "Okay," was her one word answer.

He kissed her again and then headed out of the door.

***

Elias stood in the mirror giving himself the once over. He'd dressed in a Warren Moon jersey, starched Girbaud shorts and a pair of special ordered black, purple and white Huaraches.

His co-host and partner in crime, Jacobi, was adorning himself with jewels. He knew he was fresh with his Larry Bird jersey, Roca Wear jeans and his green and white Stan Smith Adidas. After securing his diamonds in his ear, Jacobi ran his fingers through his freshly done locs that rested just below his shoulders before placing his fitted cap on his head.

It was lights, camera, *action!*

The fellas and their entourage arrived in a stretch Caddy Escalade. The turnout was lovely. The posse of ten walked past the long line and was ushered in by the owner of the club who was waiting outside for their arrival with two bottles of bubbly. And as soon as they entered, the deejay shined the spot light on them and played their intro song *Stay Fly* by The Big Tymers.

It was going down before they got there, but now it time for them to turn it all the way up. He spotted Samiyah dancing and not too far away from her was Acacia and Sleepy.

Eli pulled Samiyah off to the side. "Yo, why you brought that broad to my party?"

"Chill. I talked to her and she knows to be on her best behavior," Samiyah spoke directly into his ear, so he could hear her.

It burned him up to see her dramatic ass at his party, but he refused to let her presence ruin his night. "A'ight, Yah. Keep an eye on your girl."

Samiyah bobbed her head as she sipped from the straw of her drink. "Go enjoy your party and quit tryna check me," she giggled.

Moments later and after a few drinks were in his system, Eli began controlling the mic and two stepping while the women were selected to battle.

As each girl danced to Juvenile's *Back That Ass Up*, Jacobi walked around the floor tapping whichever female wasn't shaking hard enough. "If you can't back that ass up, then back that ass down!" As the contest continued, Jacobi dismissed over twenty competitors leaving only two to faceoff for the title of *Ms. Drop It like It's Hot*.

It was last year's champion, Kizzy, versus the newcomer, La'Tasha. Fresh flipped Cash Money's cut *I Need a Hot Girl* for the tie breaker. With the first beat, La'Tasha was all over it. She commanded the floor like she built it herself. Kizzy was gyrating her hips and bouncing her mega booty every which-a-way, but La'Tasha controlled her movements so only her curvaceous rump jumped up and down. After a while, all eyes, including the spot light, centered on La'Tasha once she landed in a split doing the ol' school *Cry Baby* dance. The people started cheering her on to the point that last year's winner was simply last year's news as La'Tasha stole the whole show.

Jacobi then escorted La'Tasha to the deejay's booth where Elias was standing, wearing an approving smile.

"So you came."

"Don't forget saw and conquered." She held her hand out.

Eli chuckled, "I like your style, boo. Straight to the point."

He reached into his pocket and pulled out a knot to peel her off five Benjis. She retrieved her winnings and thanked him, but noticed his hand was extended as well.

"Sorry. I don't give refunds."

"Don't need one, but I do need your number."

She shook her head *no.* "I don't pick up on men at clubs."

"So, how can I get to know you better if you don't give me your numerics?"

"Step your game up. I'm sure you'll figure it out." She winked her eye as she spun around and danced her way toward her girls who started a circle of attention of their own.

Jacobi heard the tail end of their conversation and burst into laughter. "Was that the sound of someone getting their faced cracked, my thuggah?"

"Knock it off," he spat. He then leaned against the wall, looking at La'Tasha who easily blew him off. But then with a devilish grin, he turned back to Jacobi. "I ain't never met a puss I couldn't tame. I'm tapping that shit. *Belee dat!*"

***

It was 2AM and the party was still jumping. Everything was co-pacetic until one girl flirted with the wrong man. *Acacia's man.*

The waitress walked up to Sleepy. "Here's a complimentary drink from that lady—right there."

Acacia snatched the drink before Sleepy could decline and she locked eyes with the woman.

She rushed in the direction of the girl whose smile turned smug instantly when she noticed Acacia bee lining her way. No sooner than the woman got out of her chair, Acacia doused the alcohol in her face and followed it with a quick push that knocked her down. She got up swiftly, but Acacia hurriedly wrapped her fingers in the woman's hair and banged her head viciously into the concrete wall repeatedly.

Elias and Jacobi noticed that people began scurrying to the other side of the club.

"What the fuck?" Elias questioned Jacobi who knew just as much as he did.

They both began pushing through the crowd to see what was going on. As they attempted to see the commotion first hand, the policemen, who were already on scene, immediately hustled their way past them to the source of the disturbance.

"Everyone, move. Move!" One officer said forcefully as people shifted out of their way.

When the boys in blue diffused the situation, Elias shook his head in disgust at Acacia being escorted outdoors, in handcuffs.

"Where is Sleepy?" She darted her eyes around the place in search of him. "Where is he?" Her screams grew louder as she frantically swiveled her head looking all around for him. The officers had a bit of a time controlling her as they led Acacia to their car because she kept pausing, forcing them to jerk her along.

"Calm down!" The policeman urged, placing her roughly in the backseat of the cruiser.

Samiyah ran up to the car and locked eyes with Acacia. *"Find Sleepy—please,"* Acacia mouthed.

Samiyah nodded her head *yes*, spun on her heels and set off to do just that. Little did she know, Sleepy had dipped out as soon as Acacia flipped out. There was no talking to her and finally enough was enough.

After ten minutes, Samiyah located Elias and pulled him away from Jacobi. "Eli, have you seen Sleepy? I can't find him anywhere."

"Nah, but if he smart, he got the fuck up outta here."

"Come with me downtown. I need to see about bonding Acacia out."

"I ain't doing that shit, ya heard me. That's yo friend. The ho can rot there for all I care."

"Eli, don't say that."

"Why not? Did you see how she fucked your girl up?" Samiyah shook her head *no*. "I'd betcha it was over some petty possessive shit. Regardless, I can't fuck with *yo* friend on no level, no mo."

"I can't argue you on how you feel, but that's still my girl, so right or wrong, I'm gonna see what needs to be done this time."

Elias shrugged his shoulders. "Me and my boys 'bout to head to Anita's and take the party elsewhere. You sure you don't wanna come with us?"

"I can't."

"Have it your way, Yah. Get at me later."

Chapter 14

"**W**hat's the matter?" Samiyah asked as soon as she heard the hysteria in Minnie's voice.

"G'Corey left here earlier this evening and he hasn't come home yet." She looked at her wall clock. It read 4:29AM.

"What happened when you called his phone?"

"He left it here."

"What did he tell you when you last saw him?"

"Umm, that he was going to chill with friends."

"He said which friends and do you have their numbers?"

"I don't know none of that!" Minnie raised her voice, snapping unintentionally because Samiyah was asking her questions she didn't have answers to. "I'm sorry. That wasn't for you. I'm scared because I don't know what else to do. I passed by his mama's house, drove all around the city, called the jail and all the hospitals but came up with nothing." Minnie began wailing violently because she believed something serious had to have happened for him not to be home like he said. She may had been jumping the gun but it wasn't like G'Corey to not be home on or before time.

Samiyah was silent while her friend let out her frustrations. When she had calmed down a little, she said, "I am about to leave Central Lock-Up. Do you want me to pass over there?"

Minnie stopped crying just enough that her words were coherent, "Central lockup? Why are you there?"

"Acacia got arrested—*again*. She's going to sit over the weekend. There's nothing anyone can do until she sees a judge on Monday and that's if he sets a bond. So I'm leaving. Do you need me there with you?"

"No. It's already late. I'm just going to sit here, pray, and continue watching the news. I just had to call someone."

"I'm heading to Cedric's but I can stay on the phone with you until G'Corey arrives."

Minnie shook her head from side to side and whimpered into the receiver, "Okay."

***

"How in the fuck do I explain this shit?" G'Corey asked out loud once he realized the time.

Satin stirred in the sheets before turning on the bedside lamp in the hotel room. "What are you talking about, baby?" She sat up fully, reaching over to caress his back, but he abruptly stood to his feet.

He disregarded her question as he rushed to put his clothes on. He couldn't believe how careless he was to slip so far. He reached in his wallet and dropped two hundred on the table. "This will cover the room." He grabbed his phone and rushed for the door.

"Wait!" She called out. "What's your number? Hell, what's your name again?"

He frowned at her, distastefully. Then he thought about that crazy thing she did with her legs during sex and left her with his digits. Then he hauled ass out of the hotel and thought of what to say to his wife whom he was certain was worried.

***

The sound of Samiyah's phone dropping out of her hand and onto the hardwood floor startled her out of her sleep. She picked it up hurriedly. "Hello—hello." She was checking to see if Minnie was still on the line, but her battery was completely dead.

Two cups of half-drank coffee sat on the table. The television was on but the volume was low and Cedric remained asleep in the lazy-boy recliner adjacent to where she was on the sofa.

Samiyah had no idea when she fell asleep, but she needed to call Minnie back. She tip-toed out of the room in an effort to not disturb Cedric as she went into the bedroom to charge her phone.

***

The sun managed to greet Minnie while her husband still had not. Her stress manifested in throbbing aches in her back and the pounding in her head. Her stomach felt queasy, giving her bubble guts at the thought he'd never return safely. The puffiness in her eyes almost made her unrecognizable, and just when she thought she had no more tears left, she surprised herself.

She had been studying the clock all morning. Each minute was torture because she had no clue what to do as the minutes turned to hours. She would pace the floor but her body fell weak to fatigue so she sat at the window in the front of their house—waiting.

It was 6:58AM when sleep summoned her but she was shortly brought into consciousness when her phone rang.

"G'Corey?"

"No, Samiyah." Minnie didn't hide her disappointment nor did Samiyah feel played about it. "I take it he's not home."

"No. He isn't." Minnie's voice trailed off. She was hoarse from her guttural crying all night and morning long.

Minnie decided to peek through the blinds as she'd been routinely checking for him and in doing so saw an unrecognizable Cadillac parked in front of her door.

"You sound like you hadn't been to sleep at all." Samiyah observed through her groggy tone.

"Not at—"A knock on the door cut her off abruptly. "Let me call you back." She immediately hung up as she sprang to her feet.

When she swung the door open, she saw a disheveled G'Corey leaning against a man she'd never seen before.

"Good morning, ma'am." G'Corey's friend spoke as he walked inside with G'Corey on his hip.

Now that her husband was alright she was free to be upset.

The guy helped G'Corey take a seat on the sofa. "Here go his keys." He reached them out of his pocket. "He may not remember, ya heard me, but once he sober up, tell dat boy he can pick his car up from my house."

"Who are you?" Minnie scrunched her face toward the stranger in her house.

"Oh," he extended his hand. "I'm Hakeem, ya heard me."

Minnie wasn't feeling hospitable, so she barely shook his hand. "What happened?"

"That boy drank too much and I let him crash by me 'cause I couldn't let my lil' round drive like dat." He headed for the door. "Go easy on 'em," he said before leaving out, suppressing a smirk. G'Corey owed him big time.

Minnie locked the door and stalked over to her husband. She was both angry and relieved. She looked down at him with tears brimming her eyes on the verge of giving him a tongue lashing when he spoke first.

"I'm so sorry." G'Corey slurred before she could say a word.

***

Acacia banged on the plexiglass in the holding tank of Central Lock-Up alongside another woman who was trying to get the attention of the correctional guard.

"Oh, C.O.?" The lady called out between the relentless pounding.

A stout gentleman approached them. "What y'all want *now*?" He sounded disgusted.

Acacia spoke first. "I've been booked hours ago and I never got my free call."

"I'll get to you." He redirected his attention to the other lady. "And you. If you want to be let out to use the bathroom, the answer is no. Use the one behind you."

That's exactly what she wanted. She flipped him the bird and sat back down.

The one room container Acacia was detained in held at least twenty-five women. There were two narrow benches that lined both walls, a broken pay phone in the very back, and a few feet away from it, an exposed toilet.

Before he could step away fully, Acacia hit the glass again. "Don't forget me." She held her thumb and her pinky in the shape of a phone to her ear.

He shook his head and waved her off.

Twenty minutes later the man came back. "Finally!" Acacia's attitude was on ten. She followed behind him, rubbing both of her arms to heat herself up from the artic cool in the building.

She trailed behind him, past the men's holding tank. A few guys cat-called, but she paid them no mind.

"What's the number?" The correctional officer asked peevishly.

"It's 246…" The line rang repeatedly as her eyebrows furrowed in confusion. There was no reason for Sleepy not to be at home. "Can you redial it?" The same thing happened—nothing. "That was my fault, sir. Can you please dial this cell number?"

"This is your last attempt. I'm not gonna be standing here all day doing this."

Acacia wanted to curse him out, but she needed to play nice. "Thank you." The call was picked up on the second ring. "Sleepy, why weren't you answering the house phone?"

"I'm not there."

"So where are you? And where were you when I was being arrested last night for that matter?" The guard looked to her to lower her voice. "You hear me talking to you?"

"You worry about the wrong things as usual. Your focus should be on you and your situation, not me."

"One minute." The man alerted Acacia.

She wanted to interrogate Sleepy, but she had limited time. She would hit him with the full force of her unbridled rage when she made it home. She breathed deeply to calm her anger. "I have AM court tomorrow. Will you be there?"

"No. I'll be at work."

"Sleepy!" Acacia called out. She was appalled at how blasé he was being.

"Acacia we're—"

The guard pressed down the button on the phone, rudely ending the call. "Time." He announced.

Acacia's face turned beet red. She wanted to burst into a flame and set the whole place on fire. Sleepy was telling her something that no doubt would elevate her pressure, but she had no way to finish the conversation because a fake Po-Po took his uniform and badge too seriously.

Tears streamed down her face past her tight lips. Suppressing the urge to go postal was taking a toll on her breathing. She stormed back to the holding tank and stood against the wall with her arms folded angrily. *We're what?* She asked herself.

***

It was Sunday night before Gerran knew it. Two entire days had gone by since the fiasco between him and Samiyah. It disappointed him to see she hadn't called, but he was no fool. She made valid points and they were all duly noted. It was just unfortunate he felt his hands were tied.

He was on the verge of a major break into the industry *and* a major break-up at the same time. He wanted to call her but all he had were good intentions to offer. He knew something had to be sacrificed on his end, too many empty promises were already on the table.

Images flashed of someone else taking his place. The idea she might leave him started to fluster his mind and he couldn't risk that overtaking his thoughts, thoughts that needed to be centered on his important meeting with a label executive the following morning. So he turned up the volume to the track he'd been listening to in an effort to drown out any voice of guilt he was feeling.

***

It was 9AM Monday morning and Acacia sat in a cell behind a door that separated her from open court. She was dressed in an orange jumpsuit with the letters O.P.P. plastered alongside the pant leg, shackled at the feet and hands. She, along with the other group of offenders, was escorted into the courtroom. She took baby steps to her seat as she scouted the room to see who all showed up. She counted four. Isabel, her two brothers, and Samiyah. Disappointment shot across her face and weighted her shoulders.

"De La Rosa." The judge firmly pronounced her name. She stood to her feet. "You are being charged with aggravated assault." He sat up high and looked down low upon her, but nothing he said mattered. She had heard it all before. "How do you plead?"

"Guilty," she didn't contest.

"This isn't your first time before me." He reviewed her jacket. "Humph." He flipped through the pages as he glared back at a very pitiful looking Acacia. "For this excessive crime, I'm going to sentence you to three years' probation and you will remain in jail on a twenty thousand dollar bond."

Acacia stared off blankly as Isabel cried at the slam of the judge's gavel.

Coffee

Chapter 15

Minnie had been unusually quiet. She didn't know how to process the explanation G'Corey had given her the previous morning. On one hand she wrestled with the legitimacy of his reasoning and on the other, she simply questioned herself.

"I had no intentions of staying out." He reached out to touch her, but she retreated her hand. "You know I don't do no shit like that. I wish I could tell you what happened, but I can't recall. Last thing I remember," he looked up at the ceiling for an answer, "I don't even remember."
"Why didn't you call me?"
"I accidently left my phone here. I could have used one of my boy's phone, but I couldn't remember your number for all the liquor I drank. Listen, I'm never getting that messed up again. That's my word."

Minnie's gut screamed not to believe him, but she had no reason not to. It was his word and there was proof to state he lied and she couldn't say she was eager to find any either. So she attributed the nagging feeling of suspicion to her insecurities and decided to let it go.
"What would you like for breakfast?" She broke her quietness.
G'Corey spent the day before making small talk with his wife and even though she kindly responded, he knew it wasn't genuine. He never liked when she was stunned to silence by any of his knucklehead actions because he needed to have someone who would love him in his corner, and Minnie was that woman. Everyone he came across saw him for who he truly was except her. In her book, he was the good guy, the one who saved the day and that made him feel good about himself.

Outside of life with her, he was a street hustler, a woman juggler, an overall foul-up by nature. But one day when he was finished with all of the shenanigans, he needed a good girl on his team. Making things right, although he ultimately lived wrong, was important to him.

"I should be asking you that question." She made an attempt to get out of the bed to head toward the kitchen anyway, but he tugged at her arm. "Lay here with me for a little while. I'll make breakfast in a bit."

"You don't know how to cook, though."

"I'll try."

Minnie softened under his gaze and lay facing him. She looked at him intently as if the sincerity that poured from his eyes would drown the eerie feeling that still lingered. But when he kissed her forehead, she couldn't help but push those thoughts to the side.

Her heart said, *There's no way a man as loving and sensitive as him would ever do anything malicious to you.*

Her gut said, *Don't go listening to that fool of a heart.*

"Shut up!" She defiantly told her gut out loud.

"Huh?" G'Corey was puzzled.

"Nothing. Just kiss me again.

What are you doing, Minnie? Don't do this, Minnie! Her gut screamed out to her, but she refused to listen.

She didn't want to be at odds with her husband. So if loving him was wrong, she'd deal with it.

He kissed her like she asked, like he wanted. He climbed on top of her. And just like that—all was forgiven.

***

When Gerran got out of his 10AM meeting with Sony, he instinctually called Samiyah. As soon as she answered, he happily shared his news. "Baby, I signed a sweet deal with the distribution company."

"Good for you," she spoke blandly.

"That's it?" He heard his air escaping his burst bubble. "Good for me?"

"What type of reception were you looking to get? I haven't heard from you since I stormed out of your place. You have no idea what has happened over this weekend nor do you care, obviously, because this was a self-serving call."

"Don't make me out to be a villain. You didn't call either."

"I'm not gonna go there with you." Samiyah had no desire or energy to tongue wrestle.

"Nah, we doin' this. You ever thought maybe I didn't call on purpose and I was giving you time to calm down."

"Don't you get it? *Time* is the problem, you give me too much time to myself."

"So what do you seriously expect me to do?"

"I *expected* you to keep your word. But now I can't say I expect anything."

"I can tell you what *I* didn't expect—" He stopped himself, abruptly. There was silence on the line before he resumed more sympathetically. "Are we that disconnected?" He now sat parked in his car.

"Yes. We. Are." She spoke slowly so her words would not be misunderstood.

"I'm sorry about Friday night. I shouldn't have let you leave, and I damn sure shouldn't have let all this time pass by without checking on you." He paused as a thought formulated in his mind. "I have an idea, let's get together today?"

"How 'bout we not. I'm not your Johnny-on-the-spot. And besides that, I have plans already."

"Like what?" Gerran was confused because she persistently argued for spontaneity.

"Does it matter? Look, you don't get to dictate when things happen. You have forced me to create a life outside of you and now you

139

want me to pop back into yours because you said so? No! It doesn't work like that."

"Okay, well since you know everything, how is this supposed to work, then?"

"Be here for me when *I*," she stressed, "need you." Her other line beeped. "I have call coming in. I will talk to you later."

"Just like that? Gerran was taken aback by her dismissive attitude.

"Just like that. Bye." She disconnected her call with Gerran and clicked over to Cedric.

"Step outside for minute." Cedric instructed the moment she said hello.

"What are you up to?" She happily climbed from under the covers on her sofa, walked to the front of her house and opened the door only to discover Cedric wasn't standing there.

But what was were her favorite bouquet of flowers, Amethyst Calla Lilies with an envelope attached. She smiled as she bent down to pick up the clear, square vase. "Okay, I am officially blushing. What's the occasion?"

"Just because."

"That's so sweet." She whiffed the arrangement. "Why didn't you stick around?"

"I'm on my lunch break and I only had just enough time to make you smile. Did I do that?"

"You sure did." She couldn't stop grinning. Then Samiyah opened the envelope to read the card, but there wasn't one. Inside was five one hundred dollar bills. "Cedric? What is the money for?"

"You told me ya girl in jail, right?"

"Yes, but I was only telling you, not implying that you help. You didn't have that to do."

"I know, sweetie." He got out of his work truck as he headed back into the building.

140

She walked back inside and placed the flowers on her dining room table. "I want to thank you, properly. Can I see you later tonight?"

"You never have to ask?"

***

Night fell by the time the officer unlocked Acacia's cell. "Come with me." Acacia followed him to a desk where he directed her to have a seat. "Sign these forms." She anxiously did so. It had been two days too long and she was ready to get home. After the outtake processing concluded, he walked her to the exit of the building. "You're free to go."

Her mother stood outside waiting with open arms once she saw her. Isabel lovingly stroked Acacia's hair and examined her under the street light as if she had been locked away for years.

"I didn't like seeing you in there, baby." She hugged her again, but this time tighter.

"I know. Thanks for getting me out. Is Sleepy in the car waiting on me?"

"No."

"Then where is he?"

"How would I know that?"

"You're right. I need to get home, then. Where did you park?" Acacia looked around for her mother's van.

She grabbed Acacia's hand and looked at her sternly. "Get your priorities in order. You have a bondman's to see. You have to speak with your job. You still have to thank Minnie, who left work to meet me, may I add, to contribute funds. *And* Samiyah for helping me come up with the rest of your bail money. You have a list of things to do before you begin concerning yourself with Sleepy's whereabouts."

"Mama, not now. I am stressed enough." Acacia ran her hands down her tired face.

141

Isabel shook her head. "I tell you what, I am going to take you to get your business handled and what you do from there is up to you. But the next time you get in trouble, let Sleepy bail you out."

***

Elias had been contemplating whether he should make an impromptu visit to see La'Tasha, who he referred to as Dark N Lovely, since he was in the uptown area. She piqued his interest since she presented a challenge, unlike the others. He was accustomed to getting women on the spot easily, but La'Tasha's playing hard to get attitude intrigued him. He *had* to pursue her. It was a man thing and he wouldn't be denied.

He pulled up to her shop, checked himself in the rearview mirror of his truck and stepped out. He was greeted the moment he walked through the French doors of the salon.

"Good evening," one lady spoke.

"Ha you doing? Is La'Tasha in?"

"Of course. Let me call her." She retreated to one of the back rooms and reentered the main floor with La'Tasha at her side.

La'Tasha walked toward Elias, but stopped at the *sign in* sheet. "I don't see your name on *my* client's list. Who are you here to see?"

He chuckled, "I'm here to see you and I don't need any of your *salon* services." Elias insinuated something more graphic in his expression.

"Come with me." She beckoned for him to follow her to the back of the shop where her stations were. She stood him in front of a vacant chair and motioned for him to have a seat. "Elias, my time cost and if you want any of it, you must pay."

"Humph. You remember my name, huh? Is that a sign that you want Cat Daddy?"

"Bay-bae, that indicates a sign of a good ass memory, plus I only heard your name mentioned like a few dozen times the other night."

"A'ight then, what's my round's name?"

142

She shook her head and let out a hearty chuckle. "Boy, I'm not doing no roll call from your party."

"That's cool," he replied, smiling.

He then went along with her game. He stood to take off his limited edition Jays, rolled up his Coogi jeans, and plopped back down onto the plush, leather vibrating spa chair.

She made small talk as she began his pedicure, but Elias zoned out. He found himself entranced by her beauty. And it seemed every touch, sound, and body movement she made screamed good sex on repeat.

He glanced at the time. He'd been there for an hour so far. And although the pedicure was legit, he had a different purpose.

"Your place closes at eight, right?" She nodded her head *yes*. "Well, it's a quarter 'til. You wanna go somewhere private and chill? Relax a bit."

"Tempting," she hinted sarcasm, "but I will be leaving much later than that." She rolled his pants legs down when she was finished. "That will be forty dollars."

He handed her a hundred. She reached into her pocket to give him sixty back, but he waved off the change. "Keep that."

"That's mighty generous. Thank you."

"You good. So what time would you like to get together later, tonight?"

La'Tasha was definitely attracted to him, but she wasn't jumping up and down. "Who said I didn't have a lil' something *something* lined up already while you tryna strong arm my time?"

"If it's not me, then it don't count." He spoke braggadociosly. "But if your hands are tied, we'll do it like this. Lay up there and store your number in my phone. I'll call you, then can we hook up and do what you like when you free."

"I'm never free," she smiled. Then with no hesitation, she removed his phone from his hip holster and stored her number along with her name.

143

Mentally, he already felt her thickalicious thighs wrap around his waist. "I'll hit you later."

"Okay." She waved him out of the shop.

"That's your boy from last night's party, right?" One of her girls asked as soon as Eli walked out.

"That's him." La'Tasha shook her head and swayed toward the register.

"Well, you must be feeling him because you don't just hand out your number."

"I didn't give him my number. I only gave him one digit." La'Tasha smirked as she began cleaning up. "He wasn't specific. Therefore, I gave him what he stipulated, a number," she laughed.

"How you gonna play him like that?" Her friend frowned.

"Don't be questioning me!" She shot back, full of herself. "I will holla, but we do it on my terms. I heard about his *love 'em and leave 'em* rep and if baby boy wants this, he will have to earn it the *La'Tasha way*."

***

Acacia had been sitting at the kitchen table mummified for the past few hours alone and in the dark, replaying the phone call that had her devastated to silence.

"What game are you playing, Sleepy?" Acacia asked as she walked through the house and saw that he practically removed all of his things out of their home.

"No games. We're over," he said plainly.

"So you just leave? I don't have a say in this?"

"You're the cause of this. Look, I'm tired of fighting with you, justifying your actions to others, or explaining myself." Acacia attempted to interrupt him but he cut her off. "I've made my decision. It's too hard to love you."

"But you know I love you, Sleepy. I can admit I'm a handful, but you know my intentions are good. Come back home and let's work

this out. I need you." Acacia tried to hold it together, but the more he resisted the harder it became to withhold the emotional floodgates from overflowing. "I'm sorry, Sleepy. There—I said it. I'm sorry." She clutched her aching stomach with her arm. "Don't do this to us."

"Hang up, Acacia, so I won't have to." Sleepy remained firm in his resolution.

"Sleepy," she frantically called out. Weak from the realization that it was over—again. "Sleepy?" But he had disconnected. Acacia called back to back and each time she was sent directly to voicemail. "Don't do this. Don't do this." She repeated over and over as she called and he didn't answer. "Don't do this, Sleepy," she cried.

Coffee

Chapter 16

"**W**hy didn't you use your key?" Cedric kissed Samiyah upon her entry into his home. She lifted her arms to show her full hands.

"I picked up your favorite. Italian." She lifted the Nonna Mia's bag in one hand and then raised the other arm. "Heinekens for you and red wine for me." She walked into the kitchen. "I'll get this together. You set up the Scrabble board."

"Oh, you didn't learn from the last ass whippin' not to challenge me in that game?"

"You wish." She handed him a beer before disappearing again.

Fifteen minutes passed before she reappeared, this time she was looking like a different girl. She had let down her locs and took off the jogging pants and baby tee shirt she'd worn when she'd arrived. She walked into the living room holding two plates while wearing a sexy, black, lace bustier lingerie set.

"Are you hungry?"

Cedric took one look at her and sprang to his feet, showcasing a burgeoning erection. He took a plate from her hand as he tongued her hungrily.

Samiyah pulled her head back, placing a hand on his chest. "Whoa, Kemosahbee. This," she lifted the lasagna, "is dinner." She then pecked his lips. "No worries though, I *am* the dessert." She smiled coquettishly as she took a seat on the sofa.

He pointed to his bulge. "You cold as ice."

"I know," she seductively smirked.

They sat next to each other indulging in their savory dish all the while having engaging conversation. Everything felt so genuine to him. It felt like he could do them every night. What more after a long day's work did a man truly need outside of his woman? Nothing if she was Samiyah.

147

Watching her turned him on. She sat with one thigh stacked on top of the other as she bent forward to make a word of the game they just started. "Or—gasm," she called out slowly as she stuck the tip of her tongue out of her mouth.

"You'll get that, ya dig."

It was his turn. He examined the board and then used his letters to spell, "H—E—A—D."

"You'll get *that*." She shaped her mouth like an O and thrust her tongue against her cheek repeatedly.

"Damn the game, ya heard me." Cedric pulled her into his arms and they began to play wrestle. Things went from ha *ha* 'funny' to ha *ha* 'hot'.

Cedric slowed his movements and his touches took a more tantalizing turn. Samiyah stroked the back of his head as he buried his face in the crease of her neck. He rubbed his hand over her netted thigh-high stockings and up toward her exposed skin. He leaned in to kiss her as his hands steadily explored her body.

Buzz. Buzz.

He disregarded her vibrating phone until the calls became insistent. He ceased his caresses and sat back into his space. An awkward feeling consumed him. "I can't keep doing this."

"Doing what?" she asked, opening her eyes to see Gerran's face plastered on the screen of her phone.

"Pretend. I can't make-believe I'm okay with being your part-time lover. It's not working for me anymore." Gerran called again. "You gon' answer that?"

"Cedric, don't."

"Don't what? Don't ask you to make a choice in which man you truly want?" He slid in closer and locked eyes with her. "I ain't never forced your hand, but you gotta choose before I do. I don't wanna lose you Samiyah, but if you can't be all mine then I already lost."

Samiyah dropped her head and tears of confusion brimmed. When she was in Cedric's presence no one mattered, but the fear of not having Gerran despite it all was overwhelming. She felt remorseful because she couldn't let go of either one. She'd tried that already.

"I know this is fucked up, but I'll make this right. I'll make a decision." She inhaled then exhaled deeply.

"What do you want me to do in the meantime, huh?" Cedric shifted her face toward his.

Samiyah was overcome with mixed emotions. She closed her lowered eyes and shook her head side to side. Then suddenly she looked up when she had her answer. "Make love to me." She swiped her knuckles against her cheeks, removing the wetness that coated her skin.

Cedric wanted to deny her, to solidify his stance, but he couldn't defy his urges. On command he stood to his feet, slid his hands beneath her arms and lifted her up from her seated position. Her arms wrapped around his neck and her legs naturally curled around his waist. He kissed her collar bone, "I love you."

She let out a breath of guilt and pleasure then directed her lips to his ear to finally say the words he longed to hear. "I love you—two."

***

G'Corey lay in bed looking up at the ceiling and then over to the clock. Minnie would be getting up for work in an hour. Usually her eight hours away was his free time to do as he chose, but he wasn't convinced he had redeemed himself from his overnight stay with Satin.

Needing to do something to remove all possible doubt from his wife's mind, he reached over her sleeping body and grabbed her phone off of the nightstand. He scrolled through her contacts and called her one of her field supervisors.

"Sorry to call you so early. This is G'Corey. Minnie's husband."

"I know who you are, sir," Alverda happily responded.

"Minnie won't be making it in today."

149

"Is she okay?"

"She good. She just won't be in."

"That's not a problem, sir. I can manage the office. And thank you for calling."

"Alright, cool. He disconnected the call and then turned off her alarm before snuggling back underneath her.

Hours later, Minnie maneuvered beneath the sheets. She felt good and relaxed, like she'd had that *weekend in bed* kind of rest. But when she opened her eyes and saw the sun, she knew she'd overslept.

"I'm late!" She panicked as she flipped the covers off of her and scrambled to get showered.

In the midst of her frenzy, she hadn't noticed that G'Corey wasn't there or that he just walked inside. He put the takeout down walked up on Minnie frantically getting dressed.

"Where are you coming from and why did you let me sleep so late?"

"About that, you're off today."

"Huh? No, I'm never off." She buttoned down her blouse.

"I said you're off. I called in while you were asleep." He began undoing her buttons.

"You did what?" She looked at him sideways as she wore an approving smile.

"Yea, it's all good. They'll manage without you for one day. So, let me have one." Now get back in bed and let me serve you." He walked her to her side of the bed and helped her back underneath the duvet. "I'll be back."

He grabbed his food bag and stepped off into the kitchen. He then put the steak omelet he'd bought from I-Hop on a plate and brought it to her along with a cup of orange juice.

"Breakfast in bed for my love."

Minnie had no clue what her husband was up to, but she was enjoying every bit of the spoil.

***

"Do you want breakfast?" Janessa giggled as Elias massaged her nipples through her nightie.

Eli could have taken her up on her offer, but he had already been over at her house for two hours and staying with a woman for more than that felt too much like a relationship.

"I don't have that kind of time." He attempted to rise from her bed, but she gently pushed him back down. He chuckled at her aggression. "You got jokes, huh?"

She stood to her feet and patted her plump va jay jay. "Nah, I got that fiya! But seriously though, you always kite outta here as if Cindefella's ride gon' turn into a pumpkin or something at a certain time. French toast takes but a second and every man has to eat. So what do you say?"

Eli grinned at her proposition. He never made it his business to get personal with any cut buddy, but Nessa was one of the cool ones. She didn't require anything outside of their sexual get togethers, so Eli reconsidered his rule of comfort, which was never to chill and offered to extend his time. "I'll stay on one term."

"Oh, yea? What's that?"

"Cook naked."

She didn't say a word. She just pushed her spaghetti straps off of her shoulders and allowed the silk gown to girdle at her feet. She then headed toward the kitchen, twirling in her tracks to face Elias who was sitting on the bed mesmerized at her body.

"You coming?"

"Fuckin' well right I am." Eli threw on his clothes, stepped into his Timbs, grabbed his fitted, and followed behind her.

Janessa hummed a tune while preparing breakfast as Eli thumbed through the sports section of The Times Picayune.

After twenty minutes of preparation, Janessa was plating break-fast for them both. As soon as she placed his dish before him, a barrage of knocks sounded off at her door.

"Who's banging on yo door like they ATF? Ya thuggah?"

"Nah. I have no man, you know that." She answered as sweet as molasses while placing a reassuring hand on his shoulder before going to the window to peep outside.

"Open the damn door!"

Janessa frowned at the tone her sister was taking.

"You not gon' put no clothes on?" Elias shoveled scrambled eggs into his mouth.

"Nah. She really wants to come inside now."

"You wild, bruh." Eli chuckled to himself. Their sisterly rivalry was comical to him.

As soon as Janessa cracked her door and Jada saw her face, she went off.

"Why is Eli's truck parked outside yo damn house?" Jada screamed on her.

She hunched her shoulders although Jada couldn't see it from the position she took standing behind her door. "Come in. Ask him yourself."

Janessa opened her door fully and Jada took in her sister's naked body and damn near lost it. "What the fuck have you done, Janessa?"

She looked over her shoulder at Eli then down at her double D's. "I made breakfast. Why? You want some?" Her smile was conniving.

"Hell no! I want to know why you fuckin' *my* thuggah!"

Thuggah? Elias almost spit out his apple juice. "Don't lay claims on me."

She stormed past Janessa and stood directly over Elias. "Eli! What are you doing here with her?"

"Enjoying my meal until you showed up." He wiped his mouth and continued eating.

152

"Don't go checking him!" Janessa folded her arms and redirected Jada her way. "You know why he's here. We fuckin' and it's damn good, but you would know that already since he unfortunately popped you off a few times before.

"How could you be so muthafuckin' triflin'? You're my sister!"

"Tsss. Oh, I'm your sister, nah? I wasn't when you was bustin' it open for *my* boyfriend. And you knew I liked him, slut. So please tell me, how you wanna police my pussy when you had no restraints on yours?"

Jada's mouth dropped. She had no idea her sister knew what happened between her and him. Jada had no comeback, so she redirected her line of fire. "How could you cheat on me with her?"

"There has to be commitment present before cheating can occur. Besides, you got a whole man out c'here. "Why you stuntin' like dat?"

"That's not the point! You don't do no shit like this?" Jada screamed and stomped her foot.

"Nah, what I *don't* do is dramatics." Elias rose from the table and walked past both women to get to the door. "Y'all ladies can hash this out the way y'all choose. I'm out."

"You're just gonna leave like that?" Jada belted hotly.

"I'll let my actions speak, ya heard me."

"I'll holla atchu later, boo." Janessa informed him as he existed out of her door.

Before Elias could close the door all the way, a cat fight over dick that was for neither woman was in progress.

***

"Acacia, this is CeCe. Are you coming in today?" The office manager at the doctor's office where she worked called her phone.

"No, not today." Acacia spoke flatly.

CeCe knew that particular dry sound of hers. She'd worked with her for three years and had been her shoulder at times when she was going through the motions. "Is this about Sleepy?" Acacia cried at the mention of his name and CeCe exhaled. "I can only cover for you for so long, so when will you be back at work?"

"I can't think of that right now." Acacia finally composed her thoughts.

"I swear, Acacia," she huffed. "Take the rest of the week off. I will tell Dr. Shapiro something came up. But there can be no excuses come Monday, okay?"

"Umm hmm," Acacia sniffled.

"I'll check on you later."

"Don't bother. I'll be the same." Acacia hung up the phone.

She stood in the doorway of their bedroom, staring at the still made bed, heartbroken that he wasn't home. She pulled her cell out of her pocket and called him again, but just like the several hundred calls she placed before that one, Sleepy ignored it.

***

"What are you about to do?" Minnie sat nervously amongst the huge crowd at the Cat's Meow on Bourbon Street.

"Hold tight, you'll see in a minute." G'Corey made his way to the stage, told the deejay his music selection, and waited for the instrumental to play.

A familiar beat began echoing out of the speakers, then in a broken pitch, G'Corey began singing.

"I've got sunshine on a cloudy day. When it's cold outside, I've got the month of May..."

Minnie covered her mouth to muffle her laughter. Her husband couldn't carry a tune to save his life, but it was so funny to her when he tried.

Then suddenly he jumped off of the stage and made his way into the audience. He grabbed his wife's hand and proudly danced with her. She felt so giddy that she was embarrassed, so she covered her face to shield herself from all of those watchful eyes that looked on.

He put the microphone up to her lips, but all she did was giggle and bury her face in his chest.

Once the song was finished, people cheered and clapped until it was time for the next person to karaoke.

He walked over to the booth with his wife in tow, paid for the video of his performance and then they left.

"Where to now?" Minnie asked, realizing that playing hooky from work was the best idea ever. But he didn't respond, he couldn't. He just looked down at her longingly, but also as if she was a stranger to him. She smiled up at him. "What?"

He always lived by the creed, *If you find a sucker, you lick it.* But Minnie was no sucker. She was unquestioning, trusting to a fault, but definitely not a sucker and he couldn't keep playing her like one.

He spent the entire day pampering Minnie in an effort to secure his position in her heart. A place that was already his indefinitely as long as he did right by their marriage. Gazing into her eyes at that very moment, he realized what he had to do.

He kissed her in the middle of the French Quarters without explaining why he paused for so long and answered, "Home. I'm taking you home."

Coffee

Chapter 17

Bam! Bam! Bam!

Samiyah knocked on Acacia's door with great urgency. Her knocks went unanswered, but she knew Acacia was home. She had called Acacia several times and she never returned her call, which was unusual. And when Samiyah spoke to Isabel and was informed that Sleepy had left, she knew her friend would be in a fragile state of mind and there was no way she was leaving until she laid eyes on her.

"Acacia! I know you're in there!" She cupped her ear to the door to check for movement inside and when she heard something she banged harder.

It took Acacia a full five minutes before she decided to open the door, lifelessly so. Acacia leaned into Samiyah, no longer able to sustain her own weight and collapsed into her embrace.

"I got you." Samiyah stepped inside while she supported her friend as she kicked the door closed, then walking her over to the sofa.

"He's gone for good." Acacia sat with her hands folded in her lap.

Samiyah sat beside her and pressed Acacia's head into her shoulder and stroked Acacia's arm consolingly. Sleepy's absence was indeed her Kryptonite and it showed.

It was evident Acacia hadn't taken a bath based on the outfit she still had on from Elias' party the week before. Her eyes were sunken into her face, and the fact that she had Ramadan breath was a good indicator she hadn't been eating much of anything.

"I'll be back." Samiyah passed through her master bedroom and into her bathroom. She ran a hot bubble bath, grabbed Acacia, and walked her toward her room.

Acacia stopped short of her bedroom's door sill. "I'm not going in there."

"Come on." Samiyah nudged her to walk in.

Acacia spasm'd her hands in the air. "Stop! I can't. It's too painful. I can't."

Samiyah stopped like Acacia summoned her to do. She then turned her around and walked her down the hall to her guest bathroom. Acacia went in without fuss. Samiyah ran more water, then helped her out of her clothes and into the tub.

"Soak and unwind. I'll be back."

Samiyah went into the kitchen and searched through the cabinets looking to see what Acacia had that would go with the chicken breast she pulled out of the freezer and placed in the microwave to defrost. Once she decided on yellow rice and a vegetable, she went back to Acacia only to find that she hadn't moved an inch, let alone bathe. So without question, Samiyah sat on the edge of her tub and began washing Acacia herself.

After she was done with her body, she then turned on the shower and washed Acacia's hair. By the time Samiyah was done her friend looked much better.

Samiyah did the whole nine thereafter. She toweled her off, dressed her, and even brushed her hair into a pony tail once she blow dried it. Upon completing Acacia's grooming, Samiyah walked her back to the sofa and pulled the blanket over her as she retreated into the kitchen to prepare a hot meal.

Before she covered her hands in seasoning, she reached for her phone to call her man. He answered on the first ring.

"Cedric, Looks like I'm gonna stay over at Acacia's for a couple of days. She isn't doing too good."

"So dude really laid up there and left, huh?"

"Yea. But she'll shake back from it. She always does, but I can't leave until she's straight, though."

"What you need?"

"Nothing I can think of. You know I keep a bag in my trunk for overnight occasions, so I'm straight."

"Well, I'm a phone call away if you need me for anything."

"I know you are."

"A'ight, sweetie."

"I love you, baby," Samiyah said unconsciously, blushing once she realized how the words effortlessly flowed.

Cedric smiled. "I love you too, ya heard me."

Her boo had her back. There were no ifs, ands, or buts about it. There was nothing she couldn't face with him on her team aside from Gerran, but that was a monster she'd deal with another day.

An hour elapsed and finally the food was finished.

"Dinner is served." Samiyah walked into the dining room, putting the two plates in her hand down on the table. She then headed into the living room to get Acacia, but she discovered she was fast asleep.

It was apparent Acacia was sleep deprived, so she had no intentions on waking her. Gently, Samiyah stroked Acacia's hair, then kissed her on the forehead. "Good night, love."

Samiyah wrapped Acacia's dinner and put it away in the refrigerator. After she ate half of her food, she washed the dirty dishes and put them away.

Once she was done tidying up, she pulled a blanket from out of the hall closet, and curled up on the sofa opposite of her friend. She then redialed Cedric.

"What's up, sweetie?"

"Remember you asked if I needed you earlier?"

"Yea, what's up, baby?"

"I needed to hear your voice some more."

Cedric chuckled. "We on the same page, then, ya heard me. I needed to hear yo voice again, too."

Coffee

She didn't ask, but Cedric shut down his computer. He would resume work later. For now he kicked his feet up on his desk and reclined in his chair as he and Samiyah talked the night away.

***

"I go to work today, right?" Minnie checked with G'Corey.

"Yea, I didn't make no calls to your office." They both chuckled.

"I wish you did, though. Yesterday was amazing

She paused in the middle of putting on her clothes. "I promise it feels like the two weeks you're home flies by, but the month you're away goes by slower than a slug race." Minnie pouted as she leaned into his embrace.

"I know. That's why I'm considering changing careers and finding something here so I can be home with you every night." G'Corey verbalized honestly.

He'd been thinking a lot lately and he really wanted to give Minnie the kind of home life she deserved. One where he would finally leave all the loose women alone, stop the lies, get out of the dope game, and just be the husband he signed up to be.

"You mean that?" Minnie sat up.

He looked her squarely in the eyes. "I've never been more serious."

"You know we have more than enough money in the bank, plus I have my job. You can quit today and we'll be straight. So what do you say? Don't report and you won't have to say goodbye to me."

"I can't play it raw like that. I leave out today, but give me a few months, then we can kiss this offshore business adios. You think you can hold tight 'til then?"

"I most definitely can." Minnie hugged him tightly around his waist in the same manner a child would her father. "I love you so much."

"I know you do, baby and I love your lil' short ass something serious too."

160

"Why it gotta be all that?" She laughed at his clowning her height, but she was indeed midget size standing next to him at six feet tall, so he wasn't inaccurate by far.

"I would love to play around with you, baby, but I gotta raise up out of here. Give me a kiss." Minnie leaned in to peck his lips. "Nah, I want tongue, lil' mama."

Minnie angled her head and gave him an erection worthy kiss to send him on his way, but then G'Corey began unbuttoning her pants.

"What are you doing?" she asked while partially kissing him.

"I need one for the road." He now went to remove his jeans.

"But you'll be late." She climbed onto the bed.

"Let me deal with that." He climbed in bed with Minnie and gave her an encore of last night's love making.

***

Gerran's mind was racing. Samiyah hadn't answered or returned any of his calls and as he thought more on the subject, he realized she'd been drifting away from him for some time.

Had I been that busy to truly not notice?

He pushed work aside, he was unable to concentrate any further. Instead, his mind wandered to the very blunt points his mother stated in their conversation about Samiyah.

"Son, she needs your time and no amount of money will ever replace you. So, if you're not talking to her, just know someone else is. And however far she has taken her friendship with this other man is solely based on how much space you have given her to develop feelings for him."

The hardest thing for Gerran to accept was that his mother could be right. He couldn't imagine Samiyah not being there. She had been faithfully his for far too long. She'd seen the worst of him and still loved him.

He drifted back five years ago to one of the incidents that drove him to put so much of himself into his work now.

"What's the matter, baby?" Samiyah walked into the dark living room of their one bedroom apartment. She could see the silhouette of Gerran's head cradled into his hands as his elbows rested on his knees. "Gerran?" She flicked the light switch, but nothing happened. She flicked it up and down repeatedly, but still no electricity. She walked over to where he was and quietly took a seat on the floor next to him. Samiyah then placed one hand on his bicep and with the other she ran her fingers up the base of his neck and through his baby fro.

"I'm sorry," Gerran said weakly. "I'm so fuckin' sorry," he now criticized himself. He got up abruptly, removing himself from Samiyah's comfort. "I don't deserve you and you don't deserve this!"

She stood up and reached for him, but he slipped his body out of her range and started pacing back and forth.

"It's gonna be—" Samiyah was silenced by his outburst.

"No it's not!" he snapped. "How is it okay? You killin' yo'self, breaking your back cleaning up behind those nasty muthafuckas." He referred to her housekeeping job at Best Western. "Every cent of your paycheck goes into this shithole and what do I do to help? Not a damn thing because I haven't worked in months. How am I supposed to be alright with my woman taking care of me?" He slapped his hand against his chest.

Samiyah jumped and tears streamed out of her eyes, but Gerran couldn't see them for his own.

"Baby," she called out softly.

"All I had to do was pay seventy-three dollars and twenty-two cents, but I couldn't even do that shit," he scolded himself.

Samiyah rushed over to console him. "Let me go!" His voice resounded in the empty room.

"Baby, I promise everything will be okay."

"Oh, yea?" He stormed into the kitchen that was just off of the living room and wildly opened the cabinets, throwing every pack of

162

Lipton noodles and boxes of macaroni and cheese onto the floor. "Is this okay? We eating poor." He then walked a few feet into the bathroom. "This ain't toilet paper." He held the McDonald's napkins in the air against the natural light of the moon that shined through the window. "Still not convinced it's not okay?" He stooped to her eye level. "Come here." He grabbed her arm aggressively.

"Stop it, Gerran!" She called for an end to his tirade.

He brought her to their bare bedroom. "You see this?" He kicked two crates that doubled as chairs when they weren't used as storage. "We sleep on a pallet. A fuckin' pallet!" He pointed to the neatly folded comforter and sheets on the floor. His face began contorting into a painful expression, then he achingly roared. "Ahhh, I couldn't pay seventy-three dollars and twenty-two cents, Yah?" His throat choked his words and he fell to his knees. "Seventy—"

"Shhh," Samiyah kneeled in front of him and his head immediately cradled into her neck. She rubbed his back and rocked him slowly. "You know how I know it'll be okay?" She didn't wait for his response. "'Cause we have each other." She sat back on her legs and forced eye contact with him. "This can't break us. I won't allow it. We will do what we do anytime the lights go out or the water gets shut off. We will improvise. And if I have to cut back on school and work extra hours, I will."

"No, you won't. I'm gonna pay it."

"I know you will." She quickly agreed. She then directed him onto their make-shift bed. "Come here." She guided him to lay in front of her. She propped up on her elbow. "Until you get the lights on, we'll just have to think of some suitable things to do in the dark." Samiyah giggled playfully to lessen the tension.

He rolled over to face her. "This is a hard pill to keep swallowing." She nodded her head in agreement. "One day we won't struggle like this. I swear to God we won't."

He leaned forward, pressing his thumb and index finger across his eyes to wipe away the mist. Then he looked around his well-

163

equipped studio and felt crushingly unfulfilled. Work always grati-fied him, which was why he could become so enthralled in it. But tonight he wasn't. He walked over to the punching bag that sat in the corner and began throwing combinations to relieve the building stress. It wasn't working. He threw his fists in the air and let out a gruff sound before he plopped back down into the chair. He stared at his phone, he wanted to call her but he couldn't pull himself to face a truth he knew he couldn't handle.

Chapter 18

G'Corey was over at Tracie's but it was evident by his low energy and nonchalant expressions he didn't want to be. But business had to be conducted. If he was seriously going to give up everything, then he needed to come off of what he currently had and fulfill his commitment for the next shipment.

There was really no reason to stay in the game. He did it for greed not necessity. So when he weighed what would be the greater loss between money or Minnie? His wife won it, hands down. *How I couldn't see that shit before?* He questioned.

Then there were the string of women he dealt with, some more than others. However, dismissing the random ones weren't going to be a problem, it was Kawanna he had mild worries about and Tracie was his biggest concern, she'd loss everything else before she'd accept losing him.

He ran his hands down his face as he examined himself. He'd built a life on lies and now he was living in a house of cards. G'Corey sat on the sofa, staring off into nothingness as he reflected on something less stressful, like the memorable time he just shared with his wife.

Minnie looked intently at herself in the bathroom mirror. She wore a navy blue corset with matching panties that she'd bought at Frederick's. She turned around and eyed herself from behind. She despised how heavy set she was, but she had to place those self-doubting emotions to the side because as much as she hated her body, she loved him more and tonight she wanted to give him a different Minnie.

She stood in the doorway of the master suite looking more seductive than ever to G'Corey. She stared at her husband as he gazed back, appreciating the thick statuesque image that stood before him. She started to feel silly, but in that moment she made it up in her mind that she would let go of her bashfulness, if only for one night. Tonight she was going to be a little exotic.

"Baby, come here." G'Corey called out with lust in his voice and a boner in his boxers.

Moment of truth. She placed one foot in front the other and released her pinned up hair so that it fell beyond her shoulders. She stopped right at the end of the bed so he could take in the full frame he loved so much. He crawled to her and attempted to caress her body but she pushed him away, which shocked him.

"Lay back," she spoke shyly at first. When he stared at her in utter disbelief, she spoke again," I said lay back!" she repeated, but with more confidence. To her surprise, he did as he was told.

G'Corey always navigated their love ship, but tonight she was the captain and he was going to enjoy the sail. She swallowed her last bit of nerves and proceeded to motion toward him. She found herself in the same position she was in on their honeymoon, attempting to do what he strongly advised her not to. But she desired to explore all doors of pleasure with him and she wouldn't be denied. Not this time.

She removed his penis from his opening and slowly moved down toward the head while gazing at him attentively. He tensed up and opened his mouth to speak, but she placed her finger on his lips and then inside of his mouth. All he could do was succumb to whatever seductress took hold of his wife.

Minnie devoured his slope, taking G'Corey by storm. He almost reflexively stopped her, but he couldn't believe she was so damn good at giving head, something she never performed on any man.

His body shook with excitement as he mentally let go and quickly found himself caught up. He felt his cum rising beyond his control. He attempted to move, so he wouldn't explode in her mouth but she latched on, refusing his weak will to not fill her open passage with his protein blast.

"Ooooo!" G'Corey bellowed in a tone she never heard before.

166

His pleasured response encouraged her to go even further. She then removed her panties and then lay directly in front of him. He traced her leg with his fingers, preparing to return the favor and dip into her sweetness with his tongue, but she nudged him with her foot, playfully pushing him backwards.

"Just watch," she purred.

He sat back and witnessed his wife transform into something like a phenomenon. She spread her legs and began a beautiful rocking motion with her hips as she danced her fingers across her chocha. G'Corey was so turned on he found himself brewing with untamable desires to take her by force, but he stroked himself instead as she insisted that she was in charge.

Her fingers swept across her clitoris in a rapid action as she jolted her inner core with her free hand. She cried out in beautiful agony which sent G'Corey into a frenzy. And like a recently freed prisoner, he broke from his seated position and placed himself where her fingers were, sending her orgasm into hydro.

He had to enter her. There was no way he could take the agony of not. With no hands, his inflexible muscle inserted itself into her slippery sex. Minnie instinctually clamped his back tightly as he thrust inside her with a drive unmatched. She wrapped her legs around his waist forcing him to use short and steady strokes. She was thrilled because for the first time he didn't delicately love her down, instead, he fucked her good.

"Oh, Minnie, baby," he panted as he lost himself in his wife.

"G'Corey, oooh, G'Corey—"

***

"G'Corey. G'Corey!" Tracie snapped. "I have been parading around this house virtually naked since you arrived Sunday night and here it is Wednesday and you still act as if you don't want this. It has been months since we last made love and I want it." She pranced around him, showcasing her hardened nipples through her

Coffee

thin t-shirt and her oversized ass that her panties did a poor job covering. "C'mon, don't you miss this good loving?"

G'Corey remained unfazed by her constant taunting and nagging as he mentally revisited Saturday night with Minnie.

***

G'Corey was working Minnie over, he could read the writings on her face. But what he didn't catch was that the tables were about the turn. Now!

Minnie maneuvered her way from underneath him and found her way on top. She straddled him with commanding presence. The feel of her sexual freedom sent her hands over her breasts that she'd placed in her mouth as she rode her husband fiercely.

G'Corey's eyes bucked as he was in awe at how downright freaky his wife had become in the blink of an eye and how right it felt to finally share that side of him with her. Her newfound sexual confidence was bringing out the beast in him.

He held her tightly as he now flipped the script on her. He rolled her to the side and then onto her knees in the doggie style position. Then with an urge out of the blue, he lifted his hand and sent it crashing down on her butt cheek, sounding off and promoting a unique sound of pleasure from Minnie's lips. Then another. Slap. And another. Slap. He pounded away energetically and she took that work as he did.

"Aaahh, baby," she cried softly. "It hurts so good." Her voice dropped, "Don't stop!"

***

"Stop ignoring me damn it! I'm horny and I want some now!" Tracie practically yelled. She walked over to where G'Corey lay and grabbed at his dick. Still with mild demeanor, he slapped her hand away and without uttering a syllable. Tracie was fuming. "It's been too long, baby. Don't you know how bad I want it?"

***

"I want it." Minnie *teased as she was moments away from tasting G'Corey's cream filling again.*

He never envisioned the fusion of lovemaking and fucking. Either it was passionate or porn, but never one in the same. Until now. G'Corey looked at his wife with a new admiration. Minnie was freaky, tempting, nasty, and sensual all while maintaining her sophistication. Everything he never knew he wanted. Suddenly G'Corey felt something inside that told him that not only did he love her, but he was in love with her too. She was everything.

"One more time," Minnie *called out to an exhausted G'Corey.*

He smiled faintly, "Huh?" He couldn't believe she wanted more after all they had just done.

She sucked on his bottom lip and repeated slowly, "One. More. Time!"

***

"You got one mo time to act as if I can be resisted. I want you to fuck me goddamnit!" Tracie was burnt to a crisp by G'Corey disregard to pull in between her thighs. Exhausted and even embarrassed from trying, she stormed out of the living room like a brat in protest.

***

"Oh, baby, whose is it?"

"Yours, Minnie." He deep stroked. "All yours."

"You're gonna make me cum," Minnie *whined in pleasure. "Ooooh, I'm cuming, baby. I'm cum—"*

G'Corey quickened his pace as he was seconds away from reaching glory himself. "Cum for me. Cum for me. Cum for meeeeee!" He came so hard he collapsed on top of her. "Damn, I love you, baby." He kissed her lips before laying his head alongside hers.

169

"I love you."

***

"I love you!" Tracie reentered the room, screaming in her final attempt to get his attention. "I'm down for you whenever, whatever and you can't even fuck me? What? Does it turns you on for me to beg?" She squatted at his eye level. "Did that burnt, crispy, heavy duty, misshaped bitch Minnie have to beg you to fuck her like—" Tracie's words were suffocated as her relentless argument to lose her breath became a life and death fight to catch it.

That got a rise of out of him. Minnie was his heart and to hear her speak so lowly and disrespectful of her sent him into rage. G'Corey grabbed Tracie's throat with the speed of light, lifting her to her feet as he slammed her against the wall in the living room. Fear enveloped her eyes as she tried to remove the vice grip he had, but she couldn't.

"Don't you ever speak of Minnie that way, *bitch*!" He growled as he forced her head backwards ever so menacingly. G'Corey was angry and lost control of his rational thinking. "You want me to fuck you? *Fuck you?* A'ight then." Like a mad man he ripped her panties off of her breathing furiously. Then vigorously, he pulled out his dick, taking no time to rush himself inside of her. She clammed up and winched in pain, but he didn't stop his entry.

"G'Corey! Stop! Please, stop!" She strained out her words, but it didn't matter what she needed him to do. She wanted the dick and now she was getting *the dick*.

He continued forcing himself inside, ramming her now swollen vagina with no remorse as he still maintained the grip that still had her pinned against the wall by the throat.

He wanted to fuck her so violently that she'd never hint at wanting his dick inside her ever again in life.

170

"Dis what you wanted, huh? You wanted me to fuck you, huh?" He breathed hard as his pumps became rapid, harder, and most punishing. He continued that rampage for several minutes until the adrenaline rushed out the head of his penis into her aching walls. He then released her and she collapsed to the floor gasping for air and holding her throat.

She lay partially on the floor, panting and crying. "You bastard! You raped me!"

"Bitch, I didn't rape you. I fucked yo dog ass." He placed his Johnson back inside of his jeans.

Tracie remained on the floor, looking up at him tearfully. "I can't believe you raped me."

G'Corey walked over to her and squatted down before her, grabbing at her jaws as he applied slight pressure. "Say I raped you again and I'll see to it that you'll never say shit again." He threatened as he angrily mushed her face.

A lot was passing through Tracie's mind as she pulled herself off of the floor and went into the bathroom, slamming the door behind herself. G'Corey bad behavior wasn't anything new, but what triggered it bothered her.

Why would he get so bent out of shape over his ex? She questioned as she ran warm bath water to soak in with the hopes of calming her ache. *Is he? Nah, he couldn't. I would know if he was still fucking with her. Urgghh, but what if he is.*

Tracie went back in forth in her mind as she tried to understand G'Corey's attack on her for seemingly nothing. She wanted to go back out there and check him, but she knew now wasn't the time to do it.

It's gon' come to light, Tracie. Oh, don't you worry!

Coffee

Chapter 19
Six weeks later...

Elias was leaving the Daiquiri Shop on St. Charles Ave. when he spotted a woman who resembled La'Tasha, placing Dark N Lovely on his mind suddenly.

He hadn't called her since she gave him her number over a month ago, but he figured she'd waited long enough. Absence made the coochie wetter, so she'd be falling over herself for the chance to have a taste of Elias, finally.

That thought brought a smile to his face. At last, he decided to call her. He pressed send under her name but automation determined the call was invalid. When he realized what had happened, the smirk on his face was replaced with a boot in his mouth.

He thought to dismiss her in the same manner she had done him, but his pride wouldn't accept defeat. Within no time he was at her shop.

"We're closed." One of the owners stated.

"Well, I'm not a customer." Elias zoned in on La'Tasha who was tidying her area, talking with another sister.

"What are you doing, Eli? I know you heard we're closed because I heard we're closed," La'Tasha chuckled and dapped her friend who was laughing along with her.

"You got all the jokes, huh? Mannn, what type of games you play?"

"Wait a minute. Why did you just pop up? Why didn't you call me first?" La'Tasha tilted her head, smiling while she waited on his answer.

"You know damn well I couldn't call your ass."

"I see," she taunted. "It took you all that time to peep that out? You could not have wanted me as badly as you proclaimed, sir."

Fuck out of here, he thought to himself. "You dat type? You want a thuggah to chase you? 'Cause if that be the case, you got the wrong thuggah. So what's it gonna be? Either you with it or you not 'cause I don't run after no one."

"But here you are on my side of town doing what?" La'Tasha folded her arms and smiled with her eyes and lips.

Eli surveyed the shop and the ladies who were paying close attention. She was cute with a fat ass, but he wasn't 'bout to go bananas over her pussy. *Shit might be lame any-fuckin'-way*, he thought.

"Have it your way. I'm out this bitch." He saluted her swiftly like she was his superior in the service and about faced to the door.

"Come better, when you come again," La'Tasha arrogantly spoke.

Eli halted for a second, but continued his stride, unaffectedly.

That muthafucka got nerve.

Her slick comment as he walked out of her shop did it for Eli. It was game on all over again. There was no way he wasn't going to plant his imaginary flag of conquer on her punani. He was going to leave well enough alone, but she just refueled his quest to hit and quit fo'sho.

***

"Baby, I've missed you." Kawanna cooed as she excitedly waved G'Corey inside of her apartment. It had been an unusual minute since she last saw him, so she went out of her way to make tonight special. Kawanna wasn't sure of what had been going on between them, but G'Corey had placed mad distance between them that she planned on closing.

Once G'Corey stepped in, she leaned in to kiss him, but he rejected her lips and stepped to the side.

"I only came tonight because I wanted to tell you this in person. I felt I owed you that much."

"Tell me what?" Kawanna reactively asked. But she dared not to speak another syllable. Fear consumed her as she noticed his mannerisms were strangely different. His vibe was unsettling and she had enough break ups to know this was the intro to yet another outro. She held her breath.

"I only come to let you know we are over," he said flatly. "To be clear, that includes all phone calls, any naked pictures, text messages, invitations like this and most definitely sex."

"If this is about—" Kawanna stopped short in her sentence when G'Corey abruptly turned around and headed for the door. "Wait!" She almost screamed hysterically. "Wait a minute!" He looked back and his eyes followed her as she slid between the tiny space amid him and the front door. She had a plan, but she needed him to stick around for it to work. "If this is truly goodbye, please at least have dinner with me. I cooked everything I know you like, so don't think about it. Just do it on whatever love you got for me."

G'Corey intentions were to leave straightaway, but he considered her offer and decided there was no harm in it. "A'ight."

Kawanna closed and locked the door behind him, then led him into the dining room. She pulled out his seat and then walked into the kitchen to prepare their plates.

She didn't have much of an appetite considering the bomb he just dropped on her, but she had to keep her composure in order to change the shift of the sail.

What changed his mind about us? I've been everything he asked even at the expense of hurting my girl. I've been freakier lately and even gave him the threesome he begged for. Urrghh, I can't believe I watched him enjoy another woman! Hell, I haven't been vexing him about nothing, I don't think. So why the hell is he calling it quits all of a sudden? Kawanna frowned as she tried to piece things together.

Stay calm. He's tried walking away before. Just work your magic, lil' mama, and he won't go nowhere.

She sat a meal fit for king before G'Corey. His mouth watered at the smell and sight of the ten ounce T-bone steak, twice baked loaded potato, cheese broccoli casserole, and asparagus she cooked.

"Thanks, boo." He dug into the savory dish and Kawanna smiled a little.

There was little talk done during dinner. She didn't know what to say and G'Corey said all there was. To break the silence between them, Kawanna headed over to the radio and turned it onto FM 102.9. Something about the soul of old school music could change a sour mood in a room, she hoped it'd do the same for hers.

Stairway to Heaven by the O'Jays played from the stereo and G'Corey instantly closed his eyes and bobbed his head to the melody. Kawanna refilled his glass of Hennessey and smiled a little bigger when she saw him take it to the head.

An hour later, G'Corey was sitting on the sofa zoned out with a third glass of Henny while Kawanna hit the blunt before passing it back to him.

He inhaled the good, then he rolled his tongue slowly as the smoke passed through his lips. G'Corey was feeling nice. When he stood up to two step to the current song on the radio, Kawanna knew it too.

G'Corey belted the verse along with Billy Paul. "Meeeeeee annnddddd Mrs. Mrs. Jonessss. Mrs. Jones. Mrs. Jones. Mrs. Jonessss."

Kawanna stood up with him, hugged him around the waist and swayed as they sung the next line together.

"We gotta thing goin' on."

G'Corey pulled from the blunt once more, cupped his hands over his mouth and then leaned closely into Kawanna's face to blow her a gun. She inhaled to the point of choking.

Kawanna pulled her head back and coughed a few times as tears rolled down her face.

176

"Rookie," G'Corey called her before he puffed again. "You can't handle it, lil' girl."

When Kawanna got her second wind, she removed the blunt from out of his hand, placing it in the ashtray. She then got up on him, body to body, and kissed him.

G'Corey hungrily kissed her back while palming her ass, pressing her against his hardening dick.

Kawanna broke their lip lock, pushed him backwards onto the sofa and came out of her shorts and panties before she straddled his lap, kissing him some more.

G'Corey wrapped his hands around her booty as he rolled her ass on the throb of his meat through his jeans.

Things were getting hot and heavy. G'Corey had octopussy hands, touching Kawanna everywhere his hands traveled causing her clitoris to swell with excitement. "I want you inside me." Kawanna gyrated her hips in a Shakira fashion against him to remind G'Corey that her up and down was spectacular.

She raised up just enough to release his monster and began tonguing his steel from top to bottom.

Girl. Stop. Fuck. Stop. G'Corey thought to himself but was unable to verbalize it. He wanted to stop her, but every muscle was controlled by the one she was viciously slurping and all he could do was give in.

She knew how much he liked dome. His eyes rolling to the back of his skull, the constant cursing, and hair pulling told her so. But she needed to fuck him like it her last time to ensure tonight wasn't truly indeed *the last time*.

"Aaaaahhh!" G'Corey moaned the moment Kawanna replaced her kissing lips with her fuckable ones. She straddled him slowly, strategic in her moves to make him remember why they were the perfect fit. She squeezed her muscles tightly as she motioned up and down the length of his pole.

"Ooooh. Sssss." The noises were endless spilling from Kawanna's mouth. G'Corey was filling her tight space snuggly as he met her grinds with thrusts of his own.

Yes! Yes! Yes! Kawanna thought as she felt victory oozing out of the moment. It wasn't but a couple of hours ago that G'Corey was hell bent on leaving just as quickly as he came, but now they were intertwined in one another's love.

G'Corey secured her around her waist and stood up just enough to flip her over onto her back. She threw one leg across the back of the sofa and wrapped the other around him as he reentered her paradise.

"Yes, baby. This pussy is all yours." Kawanna spoke sweetly between pants as he stroked her walls deliberate and steadily.

Kawanna held G'Corey tightly as she felt passion surge through each pump. It felt unlike any other time they had sex. Although she had no complaints, before it was rough, borderline sadistic, a good old fashion fuck. But tonight he was different. He was gentle with the way he pleased her. It was sensual, slow, and satisfying.

Kawanna cried out in ecstasy as she felt her body brewing one hellava climactic wave. "I love you, baby. Ooohh, I love you."

She began to cum waterfalls. The exquisite feel of her p-muscles tightening around G'Corey's dick made him lose control. "Ah. Ahh. Ahhh!" G'Corey roared as he pumped at a quicker pace, preparing to release.

"Cum in me, baby. Cum in me, baby." Kawanna was coaching him along with the hopes he'd nut inside of her. She wanted to feel him run down her thighs instead of her throat. She wanted to feel like his lover, not his slut. No, not this time. They were experiencing a first as they lay. They were having true intimacy and nothing made love making more official than a man seeding a woman's garden.

"I'm 'bout to cum." G'Corey pre-warned her as he prepared to pull out.

She clamped her arms around him. "Cum in me. Cum in meeeee," she begged.

G'Corey shook his head *no*, but his dick said *yes*. "Grrrrr!" He bust too quickly to retract, depositing a huge load inside of her.

Fuck! I didn't wanna do that, but shit the damage done nah, G'Corey thought as he stroked the last bit of his jizz out.

Kawanna stared up at him, pulled his face into hers and kissed him on the lips. Riding the climatic wave she was on, she reiterated her devotion. "I love you, G'Corey."

He peered down at her. "I know you do, but I love my wife." G'Corey pulled out of her and fixed himself back into his boxers and jeans.

Kawanna sat up and tried covering her exposed bottom with her hands. She felt played unlike ever before. "That's some real shitty shit to say to me while inside me. You don't think I know you love her?"

"Look, I came to break *it* off, but you wanted to get broke off. So deal with it." He headed over to the table top where his keys, phone, and wallet lay. "You thought your shit was magical and it was going to change my mind, but I'm sorry. It didn't, sweetheart. The pussy is fire and I like fucking you, ya dig, but it ain't worth my home."

Kawanna was flabbergasted at his callousness. She wanted to cry but she was too stunned to do anything accept drop her mouth. When she was finally able to speak, G'Corey was already at the front door. "Get the fuck out!" She ran up on his back, pushed his hand off of the knob, so she could swing the door open herself.

G'Corey looked at her cross. "Don't let yo emotions get you fucked. You see I'm leaving." Now the tears were streaming down her face as she bite into her bottom lip to keep her mouth shut. "Good girl. Just remain quiet."

G'Corey casually inhaled the night's air and relaxed his shoulders on the exhale. *One down. One mo to go*, he smiled.

Kawanna waited for him to get midway down her steps and then she blurted, "I'm quiet now, but I won't be for long." She then re-treated inside, closed and locked her door hurriedly.

G'Corey ran back up the steps, but couldn't catch her before she slammed the door behind herself. He pounded on her door. "Bitch, you know better than to threaten me." He glared at the door for a moment and then turned around to leave. He knew she was wounded and deep down her words were empty, at least they better be.

***

"What took you so long to get here?" Tracie asked the moment G'Corey walked inside.

He just left once situation and he wasn't looking forward to get-ting into another, so he didn't bother putting up defenses. He simply answered her question. "I had loose ends to tie. Why?"

"I made dinner a long time ago. I made macaroni and pork chops, so you know tonight had to be special if I cooked."

"Yea? Well, I ain't hungry. Besides, I told you 'bout doing shit like I'm ya man."

"Well, that's what I wanted to talk to you about. The not being my man part."

G'Corey huffed in frustration. Tonight was going to be another night of her campaigning for a relationship. "The answer is no, man. What a thuggah gotta do to show you he ain't rockin' with you like that?"

"You never really gave me a chance to show you how I can love you better than any of those lame bitches you fucked with, but maybe after tonight you will."

"You ain't making any sense."

"I will if you stop cutting me off. Now, as I was saying. You are difficult and ruthlessly uncaring at times, but I rather be with you than without you. And come Friday, I think you'll see me and us being together differently."

"You talking stupid, nah." He walked into the kitchen to get a beer. "Unless you gon' be a whole new person, we will never be shit, ya heard me. You too fuckin' throwed off, bruh."

That statement twisted Tracie's lips, but she still saw a possibility. "Well, smart ass. I won't be changing, but my body will." She waited for a reply, but he didn't give one. She then walked up on him and took his hand, placing it on her stomach. "We're having a baby!"

In frozen disbelief, G'Corey dropped his beverage on the ceramic tiles and backed away as if she was suddenly plagued with Leprosy.

"How the fuck and what the hell?" His mind started racing but he couldn't put his thoughts together.

Tracie rubbed her belly. "I was shocked at first too, but it dawned on me that out of every storm there is a rainbow."

"This that shit you do for attention, right? This is a joke, right?"

"Not at all," her smile faded. "The doctor will examine me on Friday and tell *us* how far I am, but I already know when we conceived. Don't you remember?"

Fuck me! G'Corey recalled the night he savagely took the pussy. That night was to make her disconnect from him not tie them forever. "I'll be a muthafuck!"

G'Corey was motionless, almost like he wasn't in his own body. As if he was watching all four of his alter egos standing in his face bitching him out for making the stupidest, most ill thought decision of his life. He was experiencing so many emotions and not one of them were happy.

He zoned out and Tracie went on and on about pregnancy and how many more kids she wanted thereafter. She was so excited that minutes of her rambling went on before she realized he checked out. She snapped her fingers in front of his face to get his attention.

"Hey! Are you listening to anything I'm telling you? I've seen you get excited behind an all-day marathon of The A Team, surely this beats that hands down?"

"This shit is too much." He shook his head side to side.

"G'Corey?" Tracie stepped slightly to the side as he slid past her, careful not to touch her through the insignificant space allotted in the doorway of which she stood.

"I'm pregnant, not contagious, you know?" She spoke to his backside.

Hours later, G'Corey had finally fell asleep, but he was awaken when he felt Tracie's naked skin pressed against his.

"What are you doing in my room? I locked the door!"

"You did, but there's no reason for all that, now is there?" She snuggled up closer to him.

He jumped out of the bed in search of his jeans, but they were on the floor on the side of the bed Tracie was on.

"Why are you tripping? I've seen you naked before. Hint the b-a-b-y," she spelled out.

"This isn't funny, Tracie. Get the hell out and let me process this shit."

"No!" she shouted. "It might be a lot for you to digest, but get over yourself! You're a family man now and in this house mommy and daddy sleep in the same bed." She patted the empty spot where he once was.

"That's it!" G'Corey was fed up with Tracie's baby talk. He was getting a hotel for the night. "Give me my jeans." G'Corey extended his hand.

"Nope, you don't need 'em. Come to bed. I promise I won't say another word. We'll just sleep and talk about it tomorrow."

He walked around the bed and retrieved them himself, but she grabbed them too. G'Corey tugged for control, but she pulled harder. Frustrated with everything, he let go and threw his hands in the air.

182

"You childish, bruh." He reached into the closet and got another pair, then he swiped his keys and cell phones off of the nightstand before she could grab them too.

"Where are you going? Don't leave us alone. Tonight was supposed to be a good night for all of us." She was on his heels, trying to stop him from leaving.

He turned around, hotly, to face her. His grimace was menacing, his lips were balled too tightly to even say one word. Her presence irked him more so now than ever, so he had to leave. And that he did.

The sound of the door slamming behind him startled her, but she reasoned the news was a little overwhelming. He'd warm up to it later.

Tracie locked the door and then looked down at her very flat stomach. "Daddy will be back home. He just needs a little more time to adjust to the idea that *we* aren't goin' anywhere."

She somehow felt comforted by that and sashayed back into his room where she threw on one of his t-shirts and climbed back in his bed. When he came back home, she wanted him to get used to the fact that her presence in his room was going to be a permanent thing.

Fifteen minutes later...

G'Corey pulled into the parking lot of a hotel. He patted his pockets for his wallet, then he realized he left it in the jeans Tracie won possession over.

"Goddamn! Muthafuck! Son of a bitch!" G'Corey hit the steering wheel.

He glanced at the time, it was almost two in the morning. He was mentally fatigued and now his body was following suit. He refused to go back to Tracie's, so he called his homie, Hakeem. He knew he could crash on his sofa 'til morning.

I'm either gettin' money or pussy, ya heard me. Either way, I'm lovin' it and a thuggah busy, so do you.

G'Corey hung the phone up when he got his voicemail. *My fuckin' luck!*

It was too late to search for a place to lay low for the night, so he decided to head back to Kawanna's. He revved up his engine and drove there although his better judgment told him not to.

Another fifteen minutes put him in front of Kawanna's apartment. He regretted having to knock on her door, but she was the better option out of Tracie.

After a few persistent pounds, Kawanna dragged herself out of bed and looked through the peephole to discover it was G'Corey. "What you want?" She guardedly questioned him from the other side of her door. She wasn't sure if he was coming back to finish what she started.

"Look, I ain't on no *rah rah* shit. I just need to crash. Open up." Some silent seconds went by, forcing G'Corey to beg. "Please."

I knew you'd come back. Kawanna prided the power of her voodoo and let him in.

He stepped inside. "It's not what you think, a'ight?"

"A'ight," she grinned behind his back.

She cleared the throw pillows off of her sofa and gave him a blanket and a pillow to sleep on. She wanted to hug him and even apologize for her earlier outburst, but she just stared at his silhouette from a distance before retreating to her room. His being there was clearly a do over and she wasn't going to botch it up by being pushy.

"Good night, baby," she whispered as she climbed back into bed with the hopes that he'd join her.

Chapter 20

Sleep didn't come easily for Kawanna that night. She awoke wanting to desperately sit down and talk with him about his stand-offish behavior as of late and now his decision to cut ties. He promised her something worth holding on to a long time ago. He promised her him. And although that would destroy Minnie if G'Corey was to ever make good on his word, she'd come too far to give up on them, so she'd just have to make peace about the decimation of her friendship somehow.

She sat on the loveseat opposite of the sofa G'Corey was sleeping soundly on despite the shine of the sun through the blinds, watching him as she sipped her coffee.

The heart loves who the heart loves and dear God I love this man. Give me a sign that he loves me too.

In the process of thinking, Kawanna kept getting distracted by G'Corey's vibrating phone. Surely his phone has rung in the past, but these calls were relentless and this time a sickening feel developed in her belly.

After twenty minutes of ping ponging the decision whether to investigate or not, she put her drink down on the table and picked his phone up. She was about to snoop.

She quietly snuck off into her room, closed and locked the door behind herself. The phone vibrated in her hands. Looking at the screen in bewilderment, she wondered who Tracie was.

Finally, the phone activity stopped and Kawanna was able to look through it. It was clear Tracie monopolized his missed calls, so she didn't bother checking that. She went straight for his inbound text messages and read those new messages who were unsurprisingly from Tracie.

Nine messages was all Kawanna was able to stomach before she went barging through his bedroom door and into the living room.

185

"Wake up, G'Corey!" Kawanna screamed on him, shaking him to rise. "Wake up!"

"Man, what?" G'Corey's yelled sharply, disorientation present in his batting eyes.

"Who is Tracie? And did you break it off with her the way you did with me? Or is she the reason—"

"For starters, calm ya lil' ass down. And I ain't never explained shit to you before, so I ain't about to start nah." G'Corey moved past her and headed for the bathroom to take a piss.

She followed behind him and stood alongside him, waving his cell phone in his face. "It's a new day, buddy, and I want answers! According to these messages, she's pregnant. Pregnant, G'Corey? How could you do this to me? I was supposed to be the only *other* woman, G'Corey. Me!" She slapped her chest and began crying.

He flushed the toilet and then snatched his phone out of her hand. "I'm 'posed to feel sorry for you or something? Man, look, that's what yo stupid ass get. Shouldn't have looked through my goddamn phone."

G'Corey walked back into the front room, then sat down on the sofa so he could throw his Polo boots on and leave.

Kawanna shook her head in disbelief as she followed behind him, trying to hold back her tears. She opened her mouth to speak, but she couldn't find the words to say. And from the looks of things, it wouldn't matter much to him no way.

No sooner than he relished in Kawanna's brief silence, Tracie called again. In a set it off frame of mind, he answered, "What the fuck, bruh?"

"Where are you and why didn't you come home?" She screamed so loud her words were barely understandable.

"Having a baby don't mean we have a home, so chill with that bullshit."

"So, the girl wasn't lying?" Kawanna shrilled in the background. "You been cheating on me?"

186

The sound of another woman's voice set Tracie off. "What bitch are you by, G'Corey? Yo ass didn't come back home because you wanted to sleep with some ho?"

"Calm y'all asses down!" He blared into the phone while looking at Kawanna who was now in his face again.

"You wouldn't let me have your baby because of your wife, but you'll have one with her? Make her ass have an abortion too!" Kawanna screamed loud enough for her to hear as well.

"What the fuck did she just say?" Tracie wanted to be clear on what she just heard.

Fuck! I hope she didn't hear that. As much as it ate G'Corey's soul, he had to pacify Tracie a little while longer. He still needed her spot. "Tracie, I'll run everything down to you. Just let me handle some shit first, then I'll be over soon as I'm done, "A'ight?"

"Ummm hmmm," Tracie breathed fire into the phone before she hung up on him.

G'Corey stood to his feet to leave. His head was smoking and he needed to clear his mind. Before he walked out of her house and her life, he wanted to make himself crystal clear.

His voice lowered to menacing growl. "We ain't shit no mo, ya heard me. When you see me, you don't know me." He then walked up on her, intimidatingly so. "And I need not tell you what I'd do to you if Minnie gets wind of any of this. I'm understood?"

Kawanna was breathing hard as anger swelled her chest. Her lips and her fist were balled into tight knots as she glared at him through squinted eyes.

"Am I understood?" G'Corey raised his voice, scaring an answer out of her.

"Yea!" Her lips trembled as she spoke.

"Good." G'Corey left, leaving a broken woman in his wake. But her feelings didn't matter, they couldn't. *One down, two to go*, he thought as jumped in his car to handle business.

Coffee

Chapter 21

"**G**irl, I'm glad you wanted to meet up at La Madeleine's for breakfast. I love their egg and spinach quiche." Samiyah sipped her lemon water before taking a seat in the outdoor patio section of restaurant.

"Yea, I don't have to see my client until ten and since they stay close by, it didn't make sense to go back home." Seconds later, Minnie began to frown as she rapidly fanned herself.

Samiyah stood and crouched down beside her. "What's wrong? You okay?"

"I don't know. This sick feeling comes in spells and I…" Minnie bolted up from her seat and headed over to the bushes alongside the building and lurched forward.

Samiyah rushed behind her, but she had to look away while she covered her mouth to suppress her own vomit.

Minnie stood up, suddenly feeling better. She placed a hand over her mouth. "I'm gonna use the restroom real fast."

Samiyah nodded her understanding and took a seat back at their table. Moments later, their food had arrived but her appetite had left.

Samiyah was between texting Cedric and watching joggers trot on the neutral grounds of S. Carrollton in the uptown area when she noticed a very familiar car make a left turn onto St. Charles.

She whipped her head around to see if Minnie was back, so she could see what she saw. But she hadn't returned. Samiyah then sprinted to the corner to get a better eye of the driver, but the vehicle was long gone and out of sight by that point.

By the time Samiyah turned around to walk back to her table, Minnie was sitting down.

"I just saw G'Corey." Samiyah wasted no time informing Minnie.

Coffee

"Impossible. He's at work." She didn't give her response a second thought.

"Well, I know what I saw," Samiyah rebutted.

"And I know my husband. He's at work and I thought you were going to lay off him."

Samiyah rolled her eyes. "It's whatever, then." *I know who I saw*, she spoke lowly under her breath. "Anyway are you feeling better?"

"Strangely, yes."

"Ummm hmmm." Samiyah looked at her and then her stomach.

"Ummm hmmm, what?" Minnie waited for the rest.

"You're pregnant, aren't you?"

"No."

"Yes you are."

Every woman that throws up ain't pregnant," she laughed it off.

"You're right, but you are, though." Samiyah was sure of it. "Let's prove me right tonight. What time do you get off?"

"I'll be home at eight, but that won't be necessary, Yah. I'm not pregnant."

"I'll be there tonight and we shall see," Samiyah grinned.

**

Elias and Jacobi were having drinks when he noticed *her*.

"Look at this bitch." Eli gulped the remainder of his Crown.

Jacobi casually glanced over his shoulder at the *bitch* he was referring to, then he looked back at Elias. "From the sound of your voice, you haven't hit that. *Tisk, Tisk*. Need me to show you how it's done?"

Elias grumbled under his breath and ordered another drink.

La'Tasha was about to grab a seat with her girls, but altered her course when she saw Elias and company. "I'll be back," she informed her ladies. She walked over to where he was sitting at the bar top. She tapped him on his shoulder. "Hi, fellas," she spoke adorably. Jacobi swiftly nodded his head upward to speak while Elias didn't acknowledge her. She frowned at his reaction. "Are your feelings hurt, baby?" She poked out her bottom lip.

"Do I look fazed?" Elias answered, looking straight ahead at the TV.

"The dog no longer has chase in him? You weren't having fun?" Elias cut his eyes at her. "Okay, I'll admit, I can be a bit of a pill, but I don't mean anything by it. Look, why don't you give *your* number."

Elias looked at her suspiciously. "Mannnn, what you on?"

"Nothing," she spoke too innocently for his liking. She crossed her heart. "No games; no agenda."

"And no holla," Elias returned his attention back to the screen.

La'Tasha frowned. "I'm not the mackable type. I only gave you what you gave me. Good night, gentlemen." La'Tasha excused herself, wiggling her fingers to wave bye.

Elias watched her walk away and then leaned back in his seat. "She play too many fuckin' games, dawg."

"Lil' mama got you shook, huh?"

"Hell no!" He placed money on the countertop to cover their tab. "Her shit ain't dipped in diamonds."

"With that whack ass G you been throwing, you'll never know."

"Ain't shit whack 'bout me, boy. Follow me. Learn." Eli led the way through the bar to where La'Tasha sat, stopping amid her and a girlfriend.

The conversation ceased as they watched the stare down between La'Tasha and Elias. The sexual energy was undeniable on both ends, everyone at the table could feel it. And now it was time for her to recognize as well.

He assertively spoke directly in her face. "You want me to fuck you?"

Her lips parted barely, then she tilted her head slightly. "Maybe I do."

"So, what's the deal?"

"Give me your number and you'll find out when I call."

***

Samiyah was on Minnie's steps at the stroke of eight, ringing her doorbell. She held the Clear Blue pregnancy test box over her eyes so when Minnie opened the door, it'll be the first thing she noticed. She heard the locks disengage and then Minnie appeared.

"You're really serious?" Minnie said as she took the box out of her hand.

"You already know. Now, I know you can use the bathroom and if not, drink some water. Hell, run your finger under some water or whatever. Let's get this show on the road." Samiyah's excitement was obvious, but Minnie's not so much.

Minnie wanted to be, but she had high hopes in the past only to be let down tremendously, so she couldn't afford that type of disappointment by having expectations.

"I'll take this for you, but please don't make too much out of it."

"Yea, yea. Quit stalling." She ushered Minnie into her bathroom and closed the door behind her as she waited on the other side. "Pee on it real good."

"Will you leave me be?" Minnie had to stop her ranting.

"Alright. I'ma be quiet, for now."

Ten minutes elapsed and Samiyah's impatience forced her to knock. "What's taking…"

The bathroom door slowly opened. Minnie wore a straight face, holding the stick at her side. Samiyah wasn't sure how to read her look, but it couldn't be good.

"I should have dropped it when you said to. I'm sorry, Minnie. I really am." She went in to hug her.

Minnie sat on the edge of the table in front of her and held the test directly in her face. "What does this say?"

Samiyah leaned forward and saw two lines, "You're pregnant," she said calmly. Once it registered she spoke more exuberantly, "We're pregnant!" Samiyah clasped Minnie around the neck.

"I—can't," Minnie tapped at Samiyah's arm, "breath."

"Oops. My bad." Samiyah jumped to her feet. We have to celebrate. A ginger ale for you and wine for moi." She reached for her keys and purse. "I'm gonna be an aunt. Yay!"

Minnie watched Samiyah prance about with excitement all the way to her car. Then she stared back at the test result in shock. "I'm actually pregnant!"

***

Samiyah had to share the good news with Cedric. They had a side bet going on from earlier about whether or not Minnie was pregnant. And two little lines ensured Samiyah the victor. She needed to call and tell him to get ready to pay up.

She accidently called Gerran, but wasn't aware until it was his voice she heard and not Cedric's.

Samiyah?" Gerran was surprised to see her call come through. They hadn't talked in some days.

"Hey." She greeted him with a twinge of guilt, hearing the longing in his voice when he called her name.

"Baby." He cleared his throat. "Can I still call you that?"

She felt horrible. He was her man still and he shouldn't have to feel like he needed clarification on something so simple. "Of course you can."

"I don't know why you were calling, but I'm hoping it was to tell you're on your way over, so we can talk. Just me and you. Nothing else."

Samiyah didn't know how to answer him. She wasn't trying to call him, let alone see him. "I was heading home actually."

"Please don't. Come here. Look, Yah, if it's my turn to beg, then I will. I just need to see you."

The vulnerability in his voice broke her heart. She couldn't refuse him. "You don't have to beg me. I'll be there soon."

She hung up with him and instantly felt like shit. Her love affair with Cedric took over, making Gerran the other man in her life. Preparing to see him felt awkward, like she was cheating on Cedric by doing so.

How did I get here?

She called Minnie and explained why her plans were changing and rescheduled their plans to celebrate while she headed to Gerran's house.

Twenty minutes later, Samiyah sat parked in her car outside of his place, reluctant to go inside. All she could do was think about how undeserving he was to get that type of treatment from her behind his back. She leaned her forehead against the steering wheel and thought more about Gerran. He may have pulled back his time, but his love was unwavering.

"Come out here and chill with me for a minute." Gerran called her to come chill with him in the backyard.

"What's the matter, baby?" Samiyah asked as she stood alongside him.

He tugged at her arm and pulled her sideways onto his lap. "Let me hold you."

She wrapped her arms around his neck and looked up at the brightly lit stars that blanketed the deep violet skies.

"This is beautiful." She pointed upward into the night.

"So are you." He kissed her arm.

"Aww, baby." She rubbed her nose against his.

"Yah, you have struggled with me and at times I'm surprised you haven't left me for someone who could give you the world. I don't have much right now but what I do have, I will give you faithfully. I love you and for what it's worth, I will never hurt you."

194

The weighted grief of loving two men burdened her to the point of tears. She couldn't breathe and she felt awful because she was too weak to do anything about it. She turned on her headlights and placed her car in reverse, she had to leave. There was no way she was ready to face him with all of those conflicting emotions battling one another, but before she could pull out, Gerran startled her with a knock on her window. Samiyah let out a sigh and then reluctantly placed her car back into park.

She rolled down her window.

"Where are you going?" He looked closer at her. "What's the matter?" He stared directly at the waterfalls cascading down her cheeks. She shook her head side to side and turned her head away. He opened her door, turned off the ignition, and pulled her out of the car and into him. "Talk to me."

Samiyah pondered for a moment. "I've said it all before."

He grabbed her face and stooped down to meet her at eye level. "Say it again." Her refusal to speak made him believe the something bothering her was *a someone*, but he didn't voice that concern. He wasn't prepared to be confronted by a blow of that nature. He rested his chin on top of her head, held her securely while exhaling the negativity he was sensing. "I don't know what's wrong, but I'll love you through whatever you're facing. Just don't stop loving me."

"I'll always love you." She quickly responded, allowing her head to lie against his chest. And she meant that truthfully.

Hearing those words were comforting to him. It didn't bridge the distance that rested between them, but it did lower the unsettling voice that echoed loudly in his mind that there was someone else.

Coffee

Chapter 22
Christmas Eve...

Elias stood on Octavia's porch and knocked on the door just as his cell vibrated. He started not to answer when he saw the door open and how scandalous the two ladies standing before him looked as they were lustfully intertwined. But he held up one finger to answer it. "Who dis?"

"Well, Merry Christmas to you, too. This is La'Tasha." A wicked smile crept on his face. "I'll cut straight to the chase. I want to see you—tonight."

"What time and where?" Elias made approving eye contact with Octavia and the girl who oozed desire into the chill of the night.

"At my shop and I don't—like—waiting." La'Tasha sexily stated before disconnecting the line.

He looked at his phone and then back at Octavia.

Octavia stepped into his space. "Why are you over there when you should be in here with us?"

Elias weighed his choices. On one hand, there was freak nasty *Tap That TayTay* with good pussy, but a whole lot of miles. And then on the other was La'Tasha, a hard to get chick who got under his damn skin, but piqued his sexual curiosity at the same time.

No matter how he sliced it, the ladies didn't compare. Octavia would be likened to a mule and La'Tasha, a thoroughbred. The answer was oddly simple. "Change of plans." He headed down the steps.

"Wait a minute." She caught up with him, grabbing his arm. "You're leaving? Just like that?"

"Yea. Another day, lil' mama." He disarmed the alarm and opened his door to get.

She looked back to her girlfriend who already walked back inside. "Fine, then! Your loss." Octavia marched back up the steps and retreated inside.

It bet' not be, Elias thought as he shut his door and headed over to La'Tasha.

***

Samiyah left Gerran's house the other night feeling indifferent. Lately, her conscience felt the silent persecution of her infidelity while around him because her love for Cedric grew exponentially, exceeding any expectations she had for their friendship. But when she thought back on Gerran, she knew his love was the greatest and it only fell short for all the right reasons.

She was sick of being torn between the two, so something had to be done with somebody and since she clearly didn't have the heart to break Gerran's, the only obvious sacrifice was going to have to be Cedric's.

When Samiyah arrived at Cedric's house he wasn't there and she was relieved because no matter how many times she rehearsed her farewell speech, it all sounded oh so painful. Lord knows he didn't deserve to be wounded, especially during the holidays, but there was never a good time to say goodbye. So, she planned on staying until he made it home and explain things as gently as possible because it was now or never and tonight might as well be that night.

Her stomach churned the more she thought about his reaction to the breakup. Hands down, there would be no rebounding from this once she said the words *it's over* and she frightfully knew this.

Without a doubt, Samiyah knew Cedric was an awesome homie, lover, friend, but he still wasn't Gerran.

To be frank, if there was a way to hold on to both men and everything be all good, she would leave it as is. But that was a fantasy and reality required her action to make a decision.

When he comes home, just speak the truth even if your voice shakes, Samiyah coached herself as she unlocked his front door. She stepped inside and she melted as she saw a radiantly lit mini fiber optic tree light up the darkness of his hallway. In addition, there was the soulful tune of Donny Hathaway's *This Christmas* playing from his stereo, adding an element of special to his tender surprise. She stood there in front of the tree in awe. *You're too much, Cedric. You really are,* she smiled but she couldn't help but cry at the same time. His love was overwhelming and she felt she didn't deserve it, although she knew she wanted it.

Underneath the Christmas tree was a purple box, her favorite color, with a card resting on top of it that read: *Samiyah, open me! Don't open it. Don't you do it! It will only make what you have to do that much harder.*

But Samiyah's curiosity overruled her mind's advice and she opened it anyway.

Inside was a key card and a note that read: *Meet me at Redd Velvet's Bed and Breakfast suite, room 112. Bring nothing but yourself. I have everything you need. Signed, I remember.*

Cedric was such the Casanova. Redd Velvet was an exquisite experience from what she was told and reservation were hard to come by. She mentioned casually how much she wanted to rendezvous there to him once, several months ago and he indeed *remembered.*

"Awww, mannnnn! What the fuck am I supposed to do?" Samiyah was angry because she confused herself even more so. "Even when I try, I can't let go."

Think, girl. Think! She demanded of herself. *I have to be an idiot to choose Gerran over Cedric, right? Cedric made these special plans for us while Gerran made plans to further his empire out of town for the week.*

Samiyah slid down the wall until her bottom hit the floor and her bent knees touched her chest and stared at the flicker of the lights

199

until she was no longer able to make out its image for the cloud of tears in her eyes.

...And this Christmas will be a very special Christmas for meeee...

Samiyah didn't know how many times the song replayed, but each spin of the record made her feel guiltier than before.

Finally, she knew what needed to be done. She gathered herself off of the floor, cut everything off, secured his house and then headed out to meet up with the one man she now knew she couldn't do without.

***

Elias pulled up, tapped his horn and La'Tasha got in after she locked up her building.

"You're looking good." He approved of her from head to toe.

"Don't I always?" La'Tasha snooted and Elias shook his head. "Just kidding—a little," she pinched her fingers together.

Elias slouched into the seat. "Where you wanna take this? Your place or mine?"

"Are you this romantic with everyone?" She leaned over the console and fluttered her long eyelashes.

He hunched his shoulders. "Don't have to be."

"Well, tonight you do," she said in a sweet but take-charge kind of way. "How does Copeland's sound?"

Elias scrunched his face as if he smelled shit. He waited for her to speak again, but she didn't. "You serious, huh?"

"What you thought?" She looked over at his feet. "I'd be worshipping at your G Nikes? I'm clearly not missing any meals, and I'm not gonna start tonight."

He thought to do the gentleman thing. Open her door and then tell her to get the fuck out. But a meal wasn't shit to him if it meant cherry pie for dessert later. "You got a jazzy lil' mouth on you, yea."

"I know."

200

Elias explored her body for a second, licked his lips like Cool James and then checked his side mirror before pulling out.

Coffee

Chapter 23

"Lady, I don't got all night." The taxi driver instructed. He was irritated at Acacia's indecisiveness. One minute she told him to pull off, then she had him circle the block, sit there in front of the house and stare out of the window. "Come on!" He threw his elbow over the headrest to look squarely at her.

Acacia glared back, then glanced at the meter. "Here!" She shoved a fistful of twenties in his hand. "Impatient asshole."

Unbeknownst to Sleepy, Acacia found out where he had been living. She followed behind him in a cab after work a few times to surmise that much. But what she didn't know was who the house belonged to, but that was about to change.

She walked up the driveway alongside two parked vehicles, one of course was Sleepy's. She used a miniature light to peer through the window of his truck to spot check for anything that may have jumped out at her.

Periodically checking behind herself to ensure no one walked up on her, Acacia continued her inspection. For a moment, she considered going back home. She didn't want to do what ultimately pushed him away, but then she saw something that pissed her off. "Ah ha! You no good bastard," she said between pursed lips.

There was no more contemplation, she walked boldly up the front steps. Hitting the door rapidly with the base of her palm, she was careful not to stand in front of the peep hole or the window. He may not have answered if he knew it was her.

"Who is it?" Sleepy questioned when he saw no one.

She bubbled with anxiety at the sound of his voice, then she disguised her own to answer. "Claudia."

"Who?" He repeated because he didn't recognize the name, but he opened the door just the same. Then she appeared front and center with her arms folded. "What are you doing here, Acacia?" He peevishly questioned, surprised she was at his doorstep.

Acacia tried to look past him, but he guarded the entry with the mass of his body. "Where is she?"

"Who?"

"The girl in there. The one whose jacket is in your truck."

"What are talking about?"

"The. Girl!" She raised her voice loud enough to wake the dead.

"Is everything alright?" The female called out from inside of her home when she heard Acacia's disruptive tone.

"Yea. Everything's alright." He stepped outside, closing the door behind him.

"Ooh, I knew it." She walked away from him and then stood back in front of his face, pointing past him. "Who is that bitch?"

He shook his head in disappointment and disgust. "Go home."

"Who. Is. She?" She asked slowly. Angrily.

He ignored her. "I'm calling you a cab." He pulled his phone out of his pocket, but Acacia knocked it out of his hand and onto the pavement.

Sleepy was losing patience quickly. He reached down to pick it up, but she kicked it out of his reach.

"Is she the reason you don't want to come home? Is she the reason why I can't sleep in *our*," she elevated her voice, "bed because it hurts too much without you in it?"

"*You're* the reason I'm not there. You're always the fuckin' reason. So quit making an ass of yourself and go the hell home!" He loudly chastised.

Acacia's feelings were hurt to the core as she batted back her tears. "You must love her."

"Her?" Sleepy was never surprised by her imagination of things.

"Yes. The *her* in there." His blasé response heated her up. It boiled her insides for him to play coy.

She grew tired of playing his game and she searched for something, anything to help channel her pain onto him so he could feel her hurt. Her eyes wandered, settling on some bricks that lay against the neighbors' house that was apparently under construction. She sprinted over to the pile and grabbed two.

She ran back up on Sleepy and hummed the first one at him with great speed, but awkward aim. The second one was sure to hit his head, but he dodged the projectile and it went crashing into the living room window.

"What the fuck is wrong with you?" Sleepy indignantly threw his hands up.

"My heart's broke, but you not giving a fuck about that is what's wrong!"

The female angrily rushed outside with a phone in her hand. "I'm calling the police."

Acacia whipped her head in the woman's direction. "Fabiana?"

A few neighbors came outside to investigate the disturbance, drawing more attention than Acacia desired. Then a familiar car pulled up alongside the curb. Javier got out of the vehicle, looking alarmed when he saw everyone standing on his lawn. "What's happening, Fabi?" He addressed his wife.

"His jealous girlfriend is what happened." Fabiana pointed at Acacia.

Acacia then looked at Sleepy. Sleepy in turn remorsefully shook his head toward Javier for the unnecessary drama.

"Ma'mi, you can't be causing a scene in front my home. My kids are inside. You got to go."

"Don't worry, baby. I called the police," she lied. Fabiana didn't call them. She loved her cousin and she wouldn't hurt him indirectly by serving justice to his girl, even if she deserved it.

Acacia swiveled her head and saw all eyes were on her and became embarrassed. "I'm sorry. I didn't mean to." She slowly backed away from everyone as she apologized repeatedly. She felt like a fool and she looked every bit of one. Acacia turned around and bolted down the street. She ran a few blocks before she stopped to catch her wind and admonish herself for her irrational behavior.

"I'm never gonna get him back acting like this."

***

"Would you two be interested in any cheesecakes for dessert?" The waitress asked.

La'Tasha waited for Elias to respond, but he was distracted. He had become bored and was slowly losing interest in the idea of conquering her.

"The bill would be fine," La'Tasha replied. She then glanced over her shoulder to see who had his attention. Then she pushed her seat back. "Excuse me for a moment."

What the fuck is she doing? Elias threw back the rest of his Crown, watching La'Tasha talk to the woman he glanced at a few times. After some hand movements and a few giggles between them, she returned.

"Here you go." She handed him a napkin.

"Huh?" Eli looked strangely at it. "What is it?" He knew what *it* was, he just wasn't sure what happened.

"I saw you watching, so I did what you were too coward to do." She tugged at his cheek like she would a baby's chubby jaw. "She thinks your shyness is cute. That might just earn you the drawers," she winked.

Eli was amazed. He was speechless. Was there really a woman who understood him? He was genuinely impressed, but he played it cool. "I'm good on that. I'm with you." He paid the bill and left a generous tip. "Let's raise up outta here."

Now it was La'Tasha's turn to be impressed. She grabbed her purse and followed closely behind him out of the door.

Once outside, they waited on valet to bring Elias' truck. La'Tasha leaned her shoulder into his. "That wasn't so bad, huh?" Elias shook his hand back and forth in mid-air as if to say it was *so so*. "Knock it off." She playfully punched him.

"A'ight, then. It was a'ight, lil' mama." He shot her a quick smile.

She watched him inconspicuously until his vehicle pulled up along the curb. She had something on her mind and it was time to let it off.

The valet gentleman opened her door for her to get inside. She tipped him and he thanked her.

Eli pulled off, stopping at the exit of the lot and looked over to La'Tasha. "Where to now? Baskin-Robbin or some shit like that?"

"Nah, my place will do."

"Word!" No other words were spoken except for the directions to her house.

Once inside, she offered him the option of getting comfortable as she retreated to her bedroom to do the same. He didn't know if she was with the games, so he was chill about the situation. He'd play it how it go.

Minutes later, she reentered the living room. Her eyes bucked when she saw only his shoes were removed and his mouth flung open when he saw all she had on were heels.

Ole girl wasn't playing after all, he thought. "A woman who knows what she wants." Eli sprung to his feet and stripped off his clothes. He was finally going to tear her ass up. He hoisted her up and then laid her on the sofa where he began his take her down.

Coffee

Chapter 24

As midnight vastly approached, Minnie curled up in her bed to watch the marathon of *A Christmas Story* for the third time that night when she heard sounds at her front door. She muted her TV to be sure it wasn't her imagination, but then she heard it again. This alarmed her. No one should have been outside of her door at that hour. G'Corey wasn't scheduled to come home for another three days, so whatever or whoever was outside of her door raised her suspicion. She didn't want to act on paranoia, but she would rather be safe than sorry. So she climbed out of bed, reached for her bat and walked slowly into the front room.

Then suddenly her door swung open, scaring a scream out of her, but it was her husband. G'Corey dropped his bags at his feet to welcome his baby girl who allowed her weapon to fall from her hand and leaped into his arms.

She kissed him fanatically, proving how much she'd been missing him before she spoke. "Oh, baby, you scared me. I wasn't expecting you."

"I know. That's what makes this even sweeter."

"You're right, but how did you manage to leave early? I didn't know you could do that."

"You can't, but a choppa came through and I got on it, ya heard me. I couldn't miss the chance to bring our first Christmas in as a married couple. I missed out on enough being out there."

Minnie stared up at him. She couldn't be more in love if she tried. Her mouth inched toward his and then she began frenching him again as she unbuckled his belt and allowed his pants to drop to his ankles.

He was just as grateful if not more to be back where he now knew he belonged. With that in mind, he picked Minnie up and pressed her back against the wall, lifting her night gown above her behind and pulling her underwear to the side in one swift motion.

It had been weeks since he felt the warmth of his woman, so he was long overdue. His dick was aching just at the thought of being inside of her hot spot. So much so, he came in mere minutes of penetration.

"Shit! I'm sorry, baby." He apologized for his quick performance as he brought her to her feet. He never minute-man'd her before.

"Baby, don't worry about that. We have a lifetime of making love ahead of us."

Minnie was as sincere as they'd came. He wanted to be like her, but he wasn't. He even thought to have a movie moment. One where he would confess his shit and promise to atone for his wrong doings. She'd cry, but she'd stay and they'd live happily ever after. But there was no way he'd get that outcome, so he abandoned the thought.

He stared at her intently and replayed her sweet words. *"We have a lifetime of love making ahead of us."*

"You promise?"

"Of course I do. I'm your wife."

"I'ma hold you to that, Mrs. Daniels."

***

"Just like that!" La'Tasha panted as Elias pinned her legs against her chest. She moaned out in bliss each time he hit her spot. "Ooh, shit! Harder. Harder. Harder!"

Sweat dripped from his body the more he pummeled her peach, sliding the sofa from its original spot and into the dining room. She sank her nails into his back as he progressively rubbed against her swollen pearl and hit her G spot.

"Ssss," Elias tucked his head into his chest to bear the sting of her scratches. *Fuckin' right,* he thought. He looked back to her, bit his bottom lip and continued to work her over.

210

La'Tasha could barely breathe, her heartbeat accelerated, and she became lightheaded. "Pick me up, quick!" She demanded. She was about to explode and she didn't want her generous release staining her expensive cashmere sofa.

She clasped her arms around his neck and he lifted her into the air, steadily bouncing her on his stiffness. Suddenly, her body tensed and her pussy muscles clamped Elias' dick with urgency.

"I'm cuming!" She nestled her head into his neck, sucking his skin with the same violent intensity of her orgasm. Her cream gushed forth like a tidal wave and the warmth of her waterfall sent Elias into a sensory overload. But it was the grip of her snatch choking his dick that made Elias cum right along with her.

"Oh, fuck!" His knees buckled, trying to sustain both of their weight under the volcanic eruption he was ejecting. He stumbled forward and then off to the side, but he managed to keep his balance.

Once he gave her the final pump, La'Tasha unwrapped her legs from around his waist and eased out of his hold. "Follow me." She curled her finger.

Elias removed the heavily loaded condom from off of his shaft, flushed it down the toilet and then shadowed her into the shower. A quick wash down was required. They were sweaty up top and sticky down below.

Five minutes later, Elias was the first to come out of the bathroom. He stretched across her bed, lying on his back with his eyes closed. He was exhausted from their nonstop hour and an half session.

La'Tasha stepped into her room a few minutes afterwards and heard him snoring lightly. She tapped his foot. "You tapping out?" La'Tasha raised an eyebrow at him.

He opened his eyes. "Never dat. I was only relaxing."

"You looked sleep to me." La'Tasha walked over to her mini refrigerator and tossed an energy drink and a jar of peanut butter to Eli. "That should give you stamina." She stood next to the nightstand, opened her goodie drawer and grabbed a handful of condoms. "*I'm* ready for round two or do you need a few minutes to get it together?"

Elias gave her the side eye, placing the items she'd given him on top of the nightstand. He stood up and pulled her into him, pressing her body against his rising nature. "I don't need that shit! Bend that ass over."

Chapter 25

Kawanna woke up Christmas morning to The Emotions playing on Q 93.

'Tis the season to be jolly, but how can I be when I have no-body...

As much as Kawanna knew she shouldn't be depressed, she was. She had been riding for him for too long with the hopes that he'd make right of a wrong he did her. But instead of being rewarded for her loyalty to him although at the betrayal to her friend, she got dropped off coldly and with no reason. She didn't understand what happened and he left that day providing her no answers.

Every man she truly loved, left. Kenneth, Chuck, Anthony, Justin, and now G'Corey. *What's wrong with me?* She needed to know. *Maybe, I'll find the answer at the bottom of this bottle.* Kawanna pitifully twisted off the cap to the Vodka and began drinking.

***

Tracie's patience was anorexic thin. Ever since the night she told G'Corey she was pregnant two weeks ago, he barely stayed home with her. And now he was on his supposed two week business run, so he told her before he left. But she knew the truth, so it ate her spirit alive.

How didn't I know and why I'm not his wife? I been his ace in the hole, his day one, his every-fuckin-thing. Not her! Tracie's feelings were crushed at the news of his marriage. When Kawanna mentioned him having a wife, she asked around and found out she wasn't lying and his misses was none other than Minnie.

When Tracie called him on being married some days later, he denied it and dared a muthafucka to challenge his lie while in front of her. Tracie didn't believe him, but in a twisted way she still loved him.

213

Entranced, her phone rang breaking her thoughts.

"Speak of the devil," she answered G'Corey's call.

"What's good, Trace?"

"You tell me."

"Don't be like that. You know my business better than anybody and I'm on one right now. But look I gotta make this quick. Black gon' be by later tonight and pick up my dry cleaning along with some bread to pay the people. Let him in to handle that. Then tomorrow he'll drop me off a new wardrobe, ya feel me?"

"He's getting everything? But why? I don't understand. Why now? Why him and not you?"

"I'll answer that when I see you in a couple weeks. Just be my soldier like we discussed and when I get back from Philly, I'll be home to put you on point, a'ight."

Tracie wasn't sure what he had up his sleeve, but she bit the bullet and went along with him. "What time?"

"Come on, nah. Just be there. I'll hit you up later. Handle that." He disconnected the line and headed back inside by Minnie. He didn't intend on shutting down his operation from by Tracie's for another month, but with his wife telling him they were expecting last night, he knew new he had to call an audible. Things were already getting too complicated.

Once his issue was out of the house, Tracie would have no leverage over him and then he could force her hand into an abortion and be done with her for good.

She stared at her phone. *Ain't nobody stupid, G'Corey.*

She then roared a rasping scream that could burst ear drums when she thought of how he was trying to play her. She was beyond furious. She was feeling wrathful and unafraid to show him such if he pushed her over the edge.

In that moment, G'Corey now had one chance to choose the family they were making before she opted to destroy the one he'd already made. Hopefully, he would make the right choice because if he didn't, he would have to put her to permanent rest to find any peace of his own.

***

"I'm going to step outside in the courtyard to get some fresh air and stretch my bones." Samiyah slipped into her jacket.

Cedric poured himself a cup of coffee. "Don't be long."

She eyed every muscle that popped across his chocolate coated skin. "I can't stay away too long." She tiptoed to kiss him before heading out of their room.

When she was a distance away from her room, she opened her phone and saw cringed when she saw all the missed calls. She didn't even bother reading the text messages.

She needed to come up with an excuse to justify why she didn't answer, but she couldn't think of one. However, she knew she had to call him now while she had a free moment because Cedric already promised her attention and adventure for the remaining of their stay.

She finally built the courage to dial his number. Each ring made her heart pound a little harder. She could only pray he didn't—

"I thought something happened to you. Why didn't you answer my calls and why you just now calling me back?" Gerran shot off rapidly the moment he picked up her call.

"I left my phone over at Acacia's and I just got it back this morning."

He didn't believe her and it was clear he couldn't ignore the eerie feeling he'd been having any longer, so he went straight in for the kill. "Who is he?" If she admitted the truth, it would kill him. But if she denied it, he would want to kill her.

"Who's who?" Samiyah knew no other way to respond. Gerran caught her completely off guard.

His blood curdled at the sign of her deflection. "The man you're with. The one you been with." It was time Samiyah found out his prolonged silence didn't make him a fool. "You've been acting strange for months. Or did you think I didn't notice? I was busy, not blind." Gerran gathered his next thoughts. "I'm not a perfect man, but I'm faithful. And for the record I'm damn sure not stupid, so answer me."

"I'm insulted you would place your trip on me. All I've done was wait on you to want me enough to do something about it."

"So let me guess, you got tired of waiting?" Gerran hemmed her up again.

"What you mean? I'm still here." Samiyah began to feel the uneasy knot in her stomach.

"You there with whoever dude is, 'cause you ain't here! And had you answered any of my calls last night, you would have known I rescheduled a show just to make it back to spend Christmas with you." So, be a woman about yours and own your shit! Tell me how you been fuckin' another man."

He was on the money calling her out like he was and there was no way to deal with it other than being truthful but that wasn't going to happen.

Her mind was paralyzed with fear and her adrenaline spiked, causing her to answer reactively. "Fuck you, Gerran, if you think it's like that!" She hung up the phone, trembling so hard her teeth chattered. Then the weight of her action weighed in.

Oh, God! What have I done?

***

Delight called Kawanna all morning long. It was unusual for her not to answer any of her calls. Delight knew she had been in a bit of funk for a couple weeks over G'Corey, which was why she promised to get her out of the house so she wouldn't be alone on Christmas Day.

But after so many hours of no response, she grew worried and decided to show up at her apartment.

She could hear Al Green's *How Do You Mend a Broken Heart* playing loudly from the stereo in her room as she drew closer to her door. She twisted her lips and pounded against the door to get her attention, but the blare of the music muffled any thuds her banging could do. Unsuccessful at getting Kawanna to open up, Delight checked under her potted plant to see if she still left her spare key there. To her relief, it was. She unlocked the door and headed straight to her bedroom. She found her sprawled across her bed with an empty bottle of Vodka alongside her.

Delight turned off the music. She couldn't help but feel disgusted that she was tripping so hard over him. "Kawanna!" Delight screamed on her, irritated that she drank herself into a stupor. "Kawanna, get your ass up!" She shook her, but she was unresponsive.

Something wasn't right. Now in a panic, Delight slapped her face a few times, trying to shock her into consciousness. "Kawanna!" Delight's voice shook. "Wake up!"

When she couldn't get a reaction from her, she started to become hysterical. She immediately checked for a pulse, but couldn't find one. That's when she noticed the empty bottle of Unisom on her side.

"Oh, shit! Shit! Shit! Shit! Shit! Shit! Shit!" In a frenzy she called 9-1-1. The moment an operator answered, she hurriedly spoke. "I need help! My cousin is dead!"

Coffee

Chapter 26

A couple of days had passed since her run in with Sleepy at Javier's. Acacia found it harder with each passing day to accept he was never coming back. It had been two months, three weeks, and one day since he'd left. That was the longest he'd ever stayed away and as a result her grieving grew strong enough to incline misery to leave *her* company. She sat on his side of the sofa, gazing outside of the window, lost in random thoughts, reminiscing.

"I don't want to live no more." Acacia threatened, curled in the corner of her room. "It's too hard living." She coughed her words through violent cries.

Isabel ushered her two younger sons past Acacia's room and ordered they play in the front yard. "Hurry!" She didn't want them to see what was happening. She reentered the room one the boys were out of the house. "Acacia, give me the razor," Isabel cried, inching toward her.

"Why did God take RJ from me?" She slapped her chest, yelping from the pain that losing her oldest brother caused.

"I don't know why, baby." Isabel shook her head as the news of Robert's murder was fresh on her grief-stricken heart. "But you can't leave me too," she spoke brokenly, reaching her hand out for the blade.

"Stop, Ma!" She shouted, extending her palm in the air. Isabel continued to creep until Acacia sliced a warning cut in her flesh, vertical to the artery in her wrist.

Isabel halted and stood frozen with fear as she watched blood trail down Acacia's arm. She was afraid any movement on her part would provoke her only daughter into joining her eldest child into an early grave.

"Acacia!" Sleepy anxiously called out the moment he bolted through the front door of her family's home. When he saw the news, he drove straight to her house. He knew she'd be there.

Carlos stood behind him in the doorway. "Upstairs," he pointed.

Sleepy ascended to the second level two steps at a time. He rushed down the hall that led to her bedroom, stopping short at the sight of his disheveled girlfriend holding a weapon in her hand. He surveyed her mother's petrified stare and then cautiously walked in.

"Acacia," he spoke calmly, taking baby steps.

Acacia wiped her eyes but they were still so heavily coated with tears that her vision was blurry. "Sleepy?"

"It's me. I'm here." Sleepy kneeled down in front of her. "Everything is gon' be alright."

"Why every man I love leaves me. First, Papi and now RJ. He wasn't supposed to leave me!" She cried each word as it passed through her lips.

Sleepy wiped her tears and she rested her head in the cup of his hand. Gently, he removed the blade. He tossed it away from them and wrapped his arms around her consolingly. Isabel fell to her knees in relief.

"I'm still here," Sleepy reassured.

Acacia cried harder and he held her tighter. "Don't ever leave me," she whimpered.

Four years passed since that day on her nineteenth birthday. The day her brother passed. The day Sleepy vowed to always love her.

Looking back on their life together, Acacia fully realized she wasn't an easy pill to swallow.

She shamefully remembered when she'd hurtfully accused Sleepy's cousin of being his out-of-town lover. She regretfully reflected on the inappropriate fight she had in Sleepy's mother's hospital room the day of her surgery over Janelle, his ex-fiancé, showing up. And she hated the unintentional wedge she'd caused between

Sleepy and his family when she suspected his mother, Ava, kept contact with Janelle so she and Sleepy would ultimately get back together. The drama that stirred as a result of everything caused a huge family feud, but Sleepy didn't abandon ship. He remained at her side regardless of how he looked to family or friends.

Reflecting on how Sleepy had always been there, choosing her when she made it difficult to do, made his absence more obvious and her loneliness unbearable. Acacia dialed his number. She hoped he'd answer but she knew he wouldn't. So she left yet another message she wasn't sure he'd listen to.

"Sleepy, I am so sad, but I understand why you refuse to talk to me. It hurts so, so, so bad, but I get it. I don't know what to say other than I apologize, and that I love you. I may have a messed up way of showing it, but you know I do. And if there is any part of you that still loves me, please come home so we can talk. Please?" She paused to suppress her cry, "*Please.*"

Acacia disconnected the call and broke down in tears. "Come home," she spoke to her phone as if it were Sleepy. She wanted the pain to stop so she reached for one of the bottles of Gin on the table before her. In an effort to numb herself, she turned it upside down and drank it as easily as she would water.

***

"We can't keep meeting like this." Eli joked as he smiled at La'Tasha's naked frame. She had invited him over for an early AM session.

She toweled off before sliding back under her duvet where Eli was awaiting. "Why not?" She batted her long lashes slowly, caressing the trail along his stomach down to his pole. "I find this to be a nice spot." She flipped the covers to expose his exquisite physique. When his nature rose at the touch of her manicured nails tracing the outline of his lower abdomen, she reached over to grab a condom.

Coffee

Seductively she rolled it onto his shaft, then she planted herself on top of him, allowing only the tip to penetrate. "Don't you like my *spot*?" She waited for an answer. He attempted to pull her downward but she energetically moved his hands. "Answer me before I—"

"Hell, yea!" He cut her off as he fully and powerfully inserted himself. He wrapped his hands around her soft ass, gripping her securely as she moved up and down.

La'Tasha rode him torturously slow and she looked sinfully sexy doing it. She smiled with her eyes and then allowed it to travel across her lips. Her sensuality turned Eli on. She rocked her hips gently, enjoying the hard thump of his pulsating dick from within.

"Ahh," La'Tasha let a small moan escape as he maneuvered his fingers over her clit. "Don't do that. You're gonna make me cum."

Elias bit his lip and scrunched his face in an effort to hold back his own release. "Fuck!" Eli panted. He thought about her cuming and how each time felt like a literal warm shower. Unable to hold back, he rolled La'Tasha over to lay between her legs and began sliding in and out of her wetness rapidly.

She stretched her legs far apart, spat on her fingers and started massaging her pearl as Elias stroked in and out at lightning speed.

"Ooo," La'Tasha bellowed. The sensation caused her back to arch.

"Mmm," Elias growled. "I'm 'bout to—"

"I'm cuming," La'Tasha carried the word like a tune to a song.

Elias continued to stroke her kitty, allowing her tightened walls to milk everything out of him. He remained inside of her a minute more before he rolled off of her and onto the other side of the bed. La'Tasha wasted no time standing to her feet. "Where are you going?" he asked.

"Need I remind you of the *don't ask don't tell* policy?" She smiled sweetly, retrieving a matching bra and panty set from her dresser drawer. "All it took was a few days of me to get you attached?"

"Not my style."

"You're so cute when you lie." She trotted off to start her shower.

"Woman, please!" He smirked as he lay back down.

Fifteen minutes later, La'Tasha came out of the bathroom to find Elias still undressed and in her bed. "Umm, sweetie," she called out softly, shaking his leg, "you gotta leave. So, come on, let's go." She kissed him.

Did she hit me with a forehead kiss? "A'ight then," he sprang to his feet. He threw on his clothes and checked himself in the mirror, smoothing over his eyebrows and goatee.

They both headed out of her house at the same time.

He disarmed his truck as she locked up. "I'll be home at nine. You can stop by then."

Two can play that game. "Sorry, Tash, but I got plans."

"Break 'em." She eased up on him, pressing her body closely to his while walking her fingers up his shirt.

Ha ha, got her! "I don't think I can, but I'll see what shakes."

"Nine," was all she said.

He tapped her luscious rump and hopped in his ride without a response. She switched her hips to her car, knowing his eyes were glued to her coke bottle image. She turned around quickly and caught him staring.

Ha ha, got him!

Coffee

Chapter 27

"**Y**ou ready to talk, nah?" Cedric asked impatiently.

She rubbed her temples. "Can it be avoided?" Samiyah asked sincerely. She had literally been sick since she hung up on Gerran. She walked out of their suite one way and returned another.

"The temperature between us changed the moment you came back inside the other morning and it's still cold as ice." Cedric was annoyed trying to figure her out. "If you don't want to be here—"

She cut him off, "I *do* want to be here."

"I can't tell," he bucked. "You're not your talkative self. Every time I've tried touching you, you've pushed me away. Nah, I'm wondering why you didn't go back to *your* place since you acting like you don't want to be bothered, ya heard me."

Without thinking Samiyah told him what was bugging her out. "Me and Gerran are over." She wasn't necessarily sure of that, but their talk felt final. Besides, there would be no recovery from the disrespect she'd shown, she was sure.

"So that was the fresh air you went outside to get." Cedric raised his eyebrows, stepped back and then chuckled in a not so funny way as he swiped his nostril with his thumb. "Lemme get this straight. I give you the world the way you want it, yet you in my face blues'd behind another thuggah? If you that bent out of shape, be with him, ya heard me."

Now was the time for Samiyah to think before she opened her mouth again. She rose to her feet and stood in front of him, placing her hands on his biceps. "Yes. I spoke with him when I stepped out and when the ugly conversation took place, it did knock the wind out of me." Cedric backed up, but she stepped forward to close the gap. "I've known and loved him a long time, Cedric. My reaction may be hurtful to you, but it's natural. However, that doesn't mean I regret being here with you. I'm where I want to be." She wrapped her arms around his waist, but he didn't hug her back. "Hug me, baby."

With his arms still at his side, he questioned sternly. "It's over?"

She looked up at him and nodded her head up and down. "It's over."

Cedric looked at her like he would a Chinese riddle before he exhaled and enclosed her in his embrace. "Fo'sho."

***

"Baby, I'm going to Winn Dixie around the corner. Do you want anything?" Minnie double checked with him before heading out.

"I'm good. What you getting, though?"

"Since New Year's around the corner, I need to pick up a head of cabbage, black eye peas, and all that good stuff before they run low on those items."

"Gotcha, but I can't think of nothing." G'Corey got off of the sofa and stood up to kiss her. "Tap the horn when you back, so I can grab those groceries. I don't want my baby mama carrying shit, ya heard me."

She nodded *yes*, then placed her hand on her stomach. "I still can't believe it's real. Everything is so good between us." She smiled, then turned to exit.

He gently patted her ass. "Hurry that ass up and get back here."

"You're crazy," she laughed as she doubled tooted her horn and pulled off.

G'Corey sat back on the sofa and cut the volume up to the weather alert warning that flashed on his screen. He listened for a second, then redirected his thoughts back to what Minnie just said. Things were good between them and they were about to get better once he heard the word from Black that everything was a go.

He swiped his car keys off of tray on the living room table, headed outside and opened the passenger door of his car. He got in, unlocked the glove compartment where he'd been stashing his second phone for more secure purposes and called Black.

G'Corey slouched back into the seat as a grin spread across his lips. He was on a natural high and he had Minnie and now the little one she was carrying to thank for that.

"What up?" Black answered.

"Yea. What up, thuggah? Say word."

"Can't do that."

G'Corey sat up quickly as if someone pushed him forward. "What you mean?"

"Tee ain't tryna see me. She refused to open the door, saying shit like get the fuck from 'round her house fo she call the cops or some shit. So, if you want it, dawg, you gon' hafta handle dat yo'self. Tee wildin'!"

G'Corey was bristling because anytime Tracie got on her level, things got complex between them. "A'ight, then. Let me call this broad. I'll holla, homie."

"A'ight." Black hung up.

G'Corey immediately called Tracie.

This bitch the main reason a thuggah will catch a case. She fuckin' stupid, he told himself as her phone rang.

"Hey, baby daddy," she answered playfully.

G'Corey wasted no time laying into her. "Bitch, who the fuck you playing with? I had my fuckin' reasons for sending my dude over yesterday," he spoke with short temperament.

"And *I* have my reasons for not letting him in." She sucked her teeth and then went in on him. "You must really think I'm stupid, huh? Like I don't know what the fuck you tryna do. I know you married, thuggah. And I know you're there with her now. I only wanted to believe shit was over with y'all and you really were out of town to re-up when you was away from me. But I'm pregnant, muthafucka, and you ain't getting rid of us like that!"

"Fuck it, ya heard me!" G'Corey decided to give her an earful. "I can't fuck with you 'cause of the petty shit you be doin' like this here and to be clear I don't give a fuck about that bastard muthafucka you carryin', so save that shit. And as for my issue, ya heard me, I'ma be there to get it and yo ass better not be on no dumb shit or—"

"Or what?" She challenged. "I'll flush and burn this shit if you don't choose your next words wisely," she threatened.

In that moment, G'Corey wrestled with blowing her brains out. The benefits of her being alive had been exhausted and it was clear she felt she was the big dog in this fight.

"Say we gon' be a family and I'll forgive you for all that bullshit you've done behind my back." Tracie meant every word. No one had to understand why she loved him, but he wasn't always cold and cruel to her. The times when they got along meant everything to her and she wanted that full-time.

Words couldn't describe how angry he was at himself for fucking with her on that level. *Give her this battle, but crush her in war*, G'Corey told himself.

Tracie was the type of female he had to shut down physically otherwise that marathon mouth of hers would never stop running.

While entranced by his rage, he heard the sound of the toilet flushing. That snapped him into the now. "What the fuck you doing?"

"You taking too long to tell me what I want to hear, so I am proving a point. I'm not fuckin' around with you. Say you're coming home now!"

G'Corey clenched his jaw repeatedly and balled his fist so tightly it ached. "I'm coming," he digressed.

"See? That wasn't hard. Just let me show you how good my love is, G'Corey. If not for me, do it for our baby."

G'Corey didn't bother fussing. He capped his frustration and answered on even tone. "A'ight, Trace. I'll be over soon."

"See you soon, baby daddy." Tracie hung up the phone with the biggest Kool-Aid grin on her face.

The moment he hung his phone up, G'Corey roared venomously. *This muthafuckin' cunt bitch!*

He sat there with his arms folded against his chest as he stared off into nothingness, plotting his next move.

Thirty minutes later, G'Corey was still sitting outside, brewing in his thoughts when Minnie arrived. He didn't realize she pulled up behind him until she tapped her horn.

G'Corey looked behind himself and saw it was his wife. He switched gears, locked his phone back into the glove compartment and met up with her by her car.

As soon as they made it inside with their groceries, the weather did a one-eighty.

"Aww, shucks! Something told me to go back in the store when I saw the dark skies, but I didn't want to get back in the line. It looks like we may need some emergency supplies for this storm that's coming." Minnie looked out of the door and into the downpour.

"I was peeping the news and they say we gon' have power outages, so you right. We will need 'em. Make a list. I'll run and get dat." His wife just provided him with the perfect excuse to leave without looking suspicious.

"No, baby. It's gloomy and I hate being alone in bad weather."

"We gon' need it, though But the sooner I leave the better, ya heard me."

Minnie couldn't argue him there. The predictions were nasty and knew those supplies were going to come in good use. "Alright, but hurry up. It's ugly out there."

Coffee

Chapter 28

A barrage of knocks at the door startled Acacia out of her drunken sleep. She looked out of the window, but it was too dark to make anything out. She groggily walked over to the door. She leaned against it for support, but when another set of knocks came she quickly became alert and stood at attention. Tiptoeing to the peephole, she was able to make out a man holding luggage.

Could it be?

"Sleepy!" She belted, fumbling over her hands to unlock the locks. She finally flung the door open and rushed into his arms.

He was caught off guard by her eagerness, but he dropped his bag and hugged her back. The rain pelting down against her face prevented her from fully taking him in, but none of that was necessary. She was finally able to reach his heart and he came home. She pulled his head down toward her for a kiss, but he resisted her advances.

"It's been too long. Please don't reject me," she panted, attempting to kiss him again. He'd come to talk, but it was clear Acacia didn't care about that. "Kiss me!"

Unable to fight the impulses, he gave in. The rain was icy against their skin but the heat between them was enough to ward off the cold. They engaged in a kiss so deeply rooted in passion tears formulated in her eyes. Sleepy *never* kissed her with such enthusiasm and it made her feel missed, loved, and desired after all.

He hoisted her up by the waist and she leaped into his hold, wrapping her legs around his frame for support. He grabbed his bag with the other hand and walked inside closing the door behind them with the push of his foot.

The house was dark, but there were no need for lights. What was about to take place between them required no sight.

***

The cracking sound of lightning was so piercing it made Minnie jump. She grabbed her phone to call her husband. He answered almost immediately.

"Baby, how much longer before you're home?"

"It's pretty bad out c'here. But once I leave Ace's Hardware, I'ma be shooting back that way. Why? What's the matter?"

"You know storms makes me paranoid."

"I know, baby. I'll be there to hold you soon, ya heard me."

"Okay." She hung up the line and curled in her bed under the covers as she waited.

G'Corey went to the store as promised and got some things for the sake of saying he truly went. He couldn't walk inside without some of the things on that list, but he also couldn't go to bed without addressing Tracie in person.

He finally pulled up in front of her door. She wanted to see him badly, and now she was definitely going to *see* him.

He envisioned caving her chest in the moment she opened her arms to hug him, then he'd step over her funky ass to clear his trap and then he'd go on about his business.

He knocked on the door and impatiently waited, but she didn't answer as quickly as usual. He knocked again more enthusiastically this time. "Tray-say," he yelled her name. Still nothing. *This lil' son of a bitch!* He reached into his pocket and pulled out his keys, but the lock wouldn't turn. It was only a matter of seconds before he realized she changed them.

The off and on again rain was on again and began crashing down viciously as he walked around the back of the house. He tried that lock too, but it was the same nothing result. He then noticed she barricaded each of the windows with bars.

While he was playing house with his wife, Tracie took the measures to protect her home from his entry. She knew he could show up at any time, get his things and leave, but he wasn't getting access without paying the toll. And she was that toll.

G'Corey was fuming mad because he had too many unanswered questions. *Why the hell would she not be here when she asked me over? Then the bitch changed the locks with my shit still inside! What the fuck she tryna prove?*

Meanwhile on the other side of town...

The taxi driver pulled onto St. Ann St. Tracie paid the fare and threw her hoodie over her head before dashing out into the thick of rain. Prior to today, Tracie never had a reason to show up at her doorstep. That was because G'Corey did a hellafied job deceiving her into thinking he and Minnie broke up a long time ago. But it was a good thing for Tracie she never discarded information that could prove to be a necessity for future purposes.

She darted up Minnie's steps and stood at her door. This was going to be the game changer for all of them. Would G'Corey be pissed? Yes. But he would have no other choice than to go home with her once Minnie kicked his ass out for everything she was about to lay on the table.

The thunder roared angrily, making Tracie's initial knocks hardly audible. But with determination she banged ruthlessly, summoning Minnie to answer.

"Come on, bitch. Answer the damn door!" Tracie shouted.

She knew G'Corey would be at her house, but he didn't know was she was at his. Tonight Minnie was going to know she meant business about G'Corey. She thought their previous run ins in the past taught her better than to mess with *her* guy, but clearly Minnie's memory was short.

The banging on her door coupled with a muffled sound of some unidentified person terrified Minnie. She redialed G'Corey, but her calls were unable to get through. She dashed to the kitchen and grabbed her butcher's knife. She wasn't sure who was beating down her door with the willpower to get in, but she prayed G'Corey made it back soon. She walked back up front cautiously just as the power suddenly went out. Minnie froze in place, petrified. In addition to the storm and the stranger at her door, now it was as dark as an eclipse.

Tracie grew angrier the longer it took Minnie to respond to her.

"Minnie!" She screamed at the top of her lungs, "Open the fuckin' door!"

Minnie heard the person this time and was able to conclude the voice belonged to a female. She looked out of the blinds, but was unable to make out an image.

"Don't be a scary bitch. Open up!" Tracie taunted, pounding away.

Anger replaced Minnie's initial fear and she began feeling for the locks on the front door only to discover the key wasn't inside of the indoor lock.

"Minnie!"

"Oh, I'm coming," Minnie announced still unable to identify the woman.

If beef is what the female was bringing, Minnie was prepared to be the butcher. She maneuvered through her house and into the bedroom in search of the key. She located her dresser and blindly felt around for it, but it wasn't in its usual place. The entire time it took Minnie to locate the key, Tracie persistently kicked and banged on the door. After several minutes of searching, Minnie found it. She walked back up front, unlocked the door, but gasped when the door was forcefully pushed open.

***

It was nearing eleven o'clock when Elias decided that he'd go over to La'Tasha's. Had he showed up for nine on the nose like she stipulated, she'd then expect he'd roll over and sit on command as well. Women like her saw that as training a man and he wasn't a Rover.

The rain had subsided, but the city was still under severe weather warnings, advising residents to stay indoors. Many streets were undrivable due to heavy flooding, causing him to make alterations to his route and creep through the streets at a snail's pace.

Finally after a thirty minute drive, he pulled up in front of her house.

"Shit!" Elias complained as he darted out of his truck and sprinted up her steps to escape the atrocious elements that started up again mid-way his drive over. "Muthafucka!" He partially wiped his face dry and examined how drenched his clothes had gotten.

He rang the doorbell and began a light bounce on his toes as the cool wind encircled him, causing him to shiver at its touch. He waited impatiently then walked over to the window to peer inside for movement. He rang the bell a second time followed up with an irritated knock. "Come on, nah. It's cold than a bitch out c'here."

The door swung open and he saw her naked image with the assistance of the multiple candles she had lit in the background, turning his scowl into a Machiavellian smile. He rubbed his hands together and placed one foot inside, but La'Tasha pressed her hand into his chest, stopping him.

"You know what time it is?" She smiled back.

He erotically pinched one of her erect nipples. "Indeed, I do." He pushed forward again, meeting the same resistance.

"I'm serious, though." She looked at him firmly.

"In case you haven't noticed, it's fuckin' freezing out c'here. Quit play—"

A man's voice boomed from the background silencing Elias in mid-sentence. "This won't go down by itself, ya know?" Her lover appeared with his dick in hand before he noticed someone at her door.

La'Tasha twisted her neck to face him. "Did I tell your fine ass to get out of bed?"

"Hurry up, then," he commanded before disappearing into the room.

Elias' brows furrowed and his eyes tightened. "How the fuck you gon' ask me to come just to have another thuggah here?"

"Easy. You forfeited your spot at 9:05. Listen, its cold standing here and we're both wet," she referred to her vaginal showers. "I'll call you."

I'll call you? Elias mentally replayed the words that stunned him to silence. He oddly found himself on the outside of a closed door with half a mind to kick that bitch in.

Pellets of rain started falling the size of knuckles and at a vicious speed. It was as if nature wanted to beat him down in case he wasn't kicking himself hard enough for stepping off of his square. He stood under her covered porch, audaciously staring between her house and the obstacle to get to his truck in utter disbelief.

"Am I gon' let this bitch play with me like *this*?"

Chapter 29

They kissed nonstop from the front door to the bedroom where she slid from his hold. He kissed her neck and squeezed her breasts, breathing heavily with anticipation. Acacia anxiously unbuckled his belt and unzipped his jeans, helping him out of his clothing. He pulled off his shirt and she removed hers as well. He traced his hands over her shoulders, down to her stomach before reaching for her panties and yanking them downward. He rose to his feet and lifted Acacia under her arms, throwing her onto the bed.

He grabbed her by her ankles and pulled her to the edge. He lifted her ass off of the bed and ran his tongue from her asshole up to the tip of her clit.

"*Sleepy*! What's gotten into you?" She moaned pleasurably.

He couldn't respond because his head was buried too deeply between her soft thighs as he speared his tongue in and out of her yoni. She cried out in ecstasy as her back arched, throwing her head back. She entangled her fingers in the coils of his hair, commanding that he keep the pace.

Acacia's body started jerking violently. "Yes! Yes! Yessss!" She was on the verge of releasing.

"Cum for me," he mumbled, circling his tongue around her clit. He then slammed his fingers inside of her rapidly, causing her to reward him with her liquid gold.

Her juices flowed heavily as if she'd never came before in life.

"Oh, my God!" She hyperventilated, attempting to regulate her breathing.

He stood to his feet and stroked himself, feeling himself hardening even more at the sight of her body squirming below.

"Spread 'em," he commanded.

Acacia opened her legs.

"Wider." His voice made her tremble. She obeyed. He ran his finger along the trail of her wetness. "Now beg me."

Acacia's head was spinning from the buzz of the alcohol and now from the aftershock of the orgasm. It all felt like one huge high.

"Fuck me, now!" She played his game.

"Not good enough."

"Please, Papi. I need you inside of me," she whined.

But he didn't budge. He only stroked himself faster.

"I want you to climb on top and slide your big dick inside my super tight pussy and fuck me blind."

"Ummm," he groaned. "That's more like it."

He placed himself on top of her, then rested the head of his dick at her opening, gently easing the tip in. Her lips parted and she let out a small breath. He bit down into her neck and plunged the rest of himself inside of her. "Oh, shit!" She called out at the moment he fully penetrated as she then dug her nails into his back.

"Urggh!" He grunted at the tantalizing sting of her scratches.

That brought out the animal in him. He removed her arms from around him and pinned them forcefully against the bed, above her head. He then maneuvered inside of her with long, quick strokes and her body tensed under the pressure of his pumps.

"Papi, it hurts," she cried in agonized pleasure.

He tried to silence her with a kiss, but her moaning grew louder.

"You're gonna make me cum," he warned.

Acacia threw her hips to meet the rhythm of his grinds. Her eruption was on its way too.

"Cum inside me."

"Inside you?" He continued to pump inside of her like a twelve gauge shotgun.

"Oohhh, I'm cuming! I'm cummiiinnnnggggg!"

The sound of her sexual roar commanded his explosion. "Aaaahhh! Shit! Aaahhhh shittt!" He boomed, feeling an immediate drain inside of her valley.

238

The way he made love to her at that moment didn't compare to anything she remembered. They didn't need to talk about why he left or why he returned home. It felt as if he'd communicated his love, longing, and remorse sexually. Body to body, she felt their souls touch.

"I'm happy you're home, Papi."

He snuggled closely into the nape of her neck and kissed her one of her spots.

No other words were spoken. She held him as he remained sprawled between her legs and they both fell asleep.

***

The sun beamed brightly and the skies were clear the next morning. It was a complete contradiction to the drear of yesterday's storm.

Having no electricity proved to work out just fine for Cedric and Samiyah. After he was completely warmed up to the idea that she was officially his girl, the bedroom games they played were intense. The kind of love they made all throughout the night was on some porno home video level.

Samiyah climbed out of the bed to use the bathroom. Casually strolling past the TV, the flat screen automatically came on.

"Oh, shit!" She laughed, clutching her chest. "That startled the piss out me, literally." She hurried to the toilet to relieve her bladder.

Cedric chuckled when he saw her jump, "It's about time shit came back on."

"I'ma start a shower. You joining me?" Samiyah asked before flushing the commode.

"Hell yea! I'm sticky and sweatier than a muthafucka." Cedric reached for the television remote to cut the power off when he saw something alarming. "Samiyah! Come here!" He urgently called her out of the bathroom.

"What?" She rushed into the bedroom over to where he stood in front of the TV. She looked to him, then turned to face the screen as he turned up the volume.

We are at the 5100 block of Bundy Rd. where we are live on the scene at Lakewind East. A fire is in progress. Firefighters are courageously making an attempt to put out this blaze…

"Oh, shit! Those are my apartments!" Samiyah hysterically shouted. "I got to go!"

"I'll drive." Cedric rushed behind her, grabbing his car keys.

***

Although the room was dark, Acacia could tell it was morning based on the small amount of sunlight that shined through the slit of her curtains. She massaged her head. She had a slight hangover, but she was too drunk in love to concentrate on it.

She happily stirred in bed involuntarily squeezing her p-muscles, feeling Sleepy's presence still between her legs. She looked over her shoulder, smiling bashfully as he lay awake looking at ease. She turned over to lay on his chest.

"Papi, I love the way you made love to me. I can tell that you enjoyed me, too."

He smiled as he turned to face her, allowing his hands to roam over her body. Then without permission, he settled back on top of her and pushed his erection inside.

"Oooh!" She gasped as he moved slowly and methodically at first, forcing her to readjust to his girth once more. She cried out loudly, holding him against her as he wrapped his arms underneath her ass to drive himself further inside of her welcoming walls.

They were five minutes into action and already lost into each other. The noises of the bed springs squeaking, her panting, and his groans drowned out the sound of her front door opening.

The unlocked door raised immediate suspicion as Sleepy entered, closing it behind him and cautiously looking around. He took notice of

240

a travel bag without peering inside, but wondered if Acacia had plans of leaving somewhere.

The sound of the door closing did little to get her attention, but it wasn't until she unmistakably heard her name that froze her movements.

"Acacia?" Sleepy called out as he cautiously looked about.

She halted, but *he* didn't. He kept breaking her down with each push. She was in a state bewilderment because she wasn't sure who she was hearing, but she needed *him* to stop so she could focus.

"Acacia?" Sleepy called out, this time closer than before.

She quietly, but rowdily pushed *him* off of her. *If that's Sleepy out there*, she processed. "Who the fuck are you?"

Still inside of her, Sleepy's identical twin brother whispered mischievously, "Diego."

Sleepy opened the bedroom door and was caught off guard.

***

Gerran had been calling Samiyah ceaselessly ever since he saw the news, which reported a severe fire that struck her complex. Each call he placed went straight to voicemail and that raised his immediate concern.

He hadn't spoken with her in a few days, but that argument didn't mean shit in lieu of what happened to her apartments and more personally what could have happened to her. He dropped everything he was doing and dashed over to her place.

Gerran broke all the traffic laws and he sped to her straightaway. A ride that would have taken him twenty minutes was made in ten. When he got there, he was able to confirm that it was her building set ablaze. That instantly broke him down. Then the worst came to mind.

What if she didn't make it out alive?

His emotions were all over the place. Although their last conversation made him feel as if he couldn't care less about her, this moment proved him wrong. He loved her much more than he could ever hate her.

He walked amongst the crowd in search of Samiyah and when he couldn't find her, he panicked. Gerran tried to get answers as to whether there were any casualties, but no one paid him any attention. He then scanned the parking lot in search of her car. When he couldn't locate it that gave him mild relief, but not much. Seeing her alive and well was what he needed.

Fifteen minutes later, Cedric pulled into the apartments, but because of the commotion and the huge crowd standing by watching, he wasn't able to get closer.

"Let me out here!" Samiyah jumped out of his car and rushed up as close to her building as she could.

She dropped down to a squatting position and began crying into her hands when she saw that one of the fires the firefighters were extinguishing was in her apartment.

Moments later, Cedric came up from behind, lifted her to her feet and immediately consoled her in his embrace.

"What am I gonna do now?" she wailed.

Cedric dried her tears with his shirt. "I got you, sweetie."

Samiyah couldn't find the solace in his consolation because the devastation was too great. But the bigger the tantrum she threw, the tighter Cedric held her to help calm her down.

"Look at me. Look at me! You not gonna go through this alone, ya heard me. Its gon' be alright. I swear I won't let you feel the brunt of this."

Her frenzy simmered just enough for her to hear him sincerely offer his support, but the tears steadily flowed like a running faucet.

He cupped her face and got her to look him in the eyes, soundlessly communicating that his shoulders were strong enough to carry her load and she had nothing to worry about. He then confirmed his silent decree with a tender kiss on her forehead and then onto her lips, but the moment of endearment was interrupted.

Gerran angrily separated Samiyah and Cedric, forcing Samiyah to stumble backwards slightly. Gerran faced Samiyah, not once giving place to Cedric who was behind regaining his footing from the shove. Gerran's eyes were bloodshot with fury. His breathing was labored and his fists were tightly balled.

Tears stained his face. "I was worried about you, and you was with a thuggah you denied having?"

Samiyah was fossilized with fear and for the first time with Gerran she was justified in feeling such an emotion. She threw her hands up and attempted to reason the situation.

Cedric assumed the mad man in front of him was Gerran based on Samiyah's reaction. So, he instinctually stepped between them, shielding Samiyah.

"You got a problem with her, you address me!" Cedric growled, shoving Gerran backwards, forcing him to stagger.

Samiyah never witnessed Cedric in a scuffle, but she could attest that Gerran was a different beast when provoked.

Gerran grimaced, shaking his head slowly as if to inaudibly tell Cedric he shouldn't have done that. Gerran then rushed him, delivering a brutal blow that connected to his jaw, followed by an uppercut that rocked him.

Cedric blinked hard and mildly shook off the hits. He recovered his stance, jabbed Gerran in the nose to daze him before he swiftly chin-checked him with a flying elbow. Next, Cedric charged him, placing Gerran in a bear hug.

Gerran attempted to get out of his hold, but he couldn't release the grip Cedric held while pinning his arms in the process. Gerran then leaned back and head-butted Cedric twice until he released him. The men began tussling back and forth, grabbing at one another in an effort to gain the upper hand.

Samiyah stood helpless, watching two men she loved fight over their love for her. "Stop them!" She pleaded to random men on the scene, but no one intervened. She tried to diffuse the brawl herself, but ended up being unintentionally, but violently pushed to the concrete.

If the fight didn't end soon, the men were bound to get the attention of the distracted police.

The crowd grew bigger as spectators appeared. Suddenly, one woman screamed and pointed. "He's got a gun!"

Samiyah's eyes bulged out of her sockets. She stood to her feet, waving her hands wildly, "Stop! No!"

To Be Continued...

Love Knows No Boundaries **II: Karma Unleashed**
Available Now!

Author's Note

Hi _____ (insert name here)

This is my first published novel and I want to truly thank you for giving me a chance. I hope you are intrigued enough to pick of the second install of this series and continue the journey of Love Knows No Boundaries with me because what lies ahead is truly unbelievable. Karma *will* be unleashed and no one will be ready!

Also, if I may request one more thing. I ask that you leave a review on Amazon regarding your reading experience. It's so important to me to know if I have served my purpose as a writer by giving you a quality product and an entertaining read. Hope you have enjoyed #LKNB so far and thank you in advance.

Sincerely,
Queen Coffee

Stay Connected with Us!

Text **LOCKDOWN** to 22828 to stay up-to-date with new releases, sneak peaks, contests and more…

Thank you!

Submission Guideline.

Submit the first three chapters of your completed manuscript to ldpsubmissions@gmail.com, subject line: Your book's title. The manuscript must be in a .doc file and sent as an attachment. Document should be in Times New Roman, double spaced and in size 12 font. Also, provide your synopsis and full contact information. If sending multiple submissions, they must each be in a separate email.

Have a story but no way to send it electronically? You can still submit to LDP/Ca$h Presents. Send in the first three chapters, written or typed, of your completed manuscript to:

LDP: Submissions Dept
Po Box 870494
Mesquite, Tx 75187

DO NOT send original manuscript. Must be a duplicate.

Provide your synopsis and a cover letter containing your full contact information.

Thanks for considering LDP and Ca$h Presents.

Coming Soon from Lock Down Publications/Ca$h Presents

BOW DOWN TO MY GANGSTA

By **Ca$h**

TORN BETWEEN TWO

By **Coffee**

BLOOD STAINS OF A SHOTTA **II**

By **Jamaica**

WHEN THE STREETS CLAP BACK **II**

By **Jibril Williams**

STEADY MOBBIN

By **Marcellus Allen**

BLOOD OF A BOSS **V**

By **Askari**

BRIDE OF A HUSTLA **III**

By **Destiny Skai**

WHEN A GOOD GIRL GOES BAD **II**

By **Adrienne**

LOVE & CHASIN' PAPER **II**

By **Qay Crockett**

THE HEART OF A GANGSTA **III**

By **Jerry Jackson**

LOYAL TO THE GAME **IV**

By **T.J. & Jelissa**

A DOPEBOY'S PRAYER **II**

Love Knows No Boundaries

By **Eddie "Wolf" Lee**

IF LOVING YOU IS WRONG... **III**

By **Jelissa**

BLOODY COMMAS **III**

SKI MASK CARTEL **II**

By **T.J. Edwards**

BLAST FOR ME **II**

RAISED AS A GOON V

BRED BY THE SLUMS

By **Ghost**

A DISTINGUISHED THUG STOLE MY HEART **III**

By **Meesha**

ADDICTIED TO THE DRAMA **II**

By **Jamila Mathis**

LIPSTICK KILLAH II

By **Mimi**

THE BOSSMAN'S DAUGHTERS 4

By **Aryanna**

Available Now

RESTRAINING ORDER **I & II**

By **CA$H & Coffee**

LOVE KNOWS NO BOUNDARIES **I II & III**

By **Coffee**

RAISED AS A GOON I, II, III & IV

249

Coffee

By **Ghost**

LAY IT DOWN **I & II**

LAST OF A DYING BREED

BLOOD STAINS OF A SHOTTA

By **Jamaica**

LOYAL TO THE GAME

LOYAL TO THE GAME II

LOYAL TO THE GAME III

By **TJ & Jelissa**

BLOODY COMMAS I & II

SKI MASK CARTEL

By **T.J. Edwards**

IF LOVING HIM IS WRONG...I & II

By **Jelissa**

WHEN THE STREETS CLAP BACK

By **Jibril Williams**

A DISTINGUISHED THUG STOLE MY HEART I & II

By **Meesha**

PUSH IT TO THE LIMIT

By **Bre' Hayes**

BLOOD OF A BOSS **I, II, III & IV**

By **Askari**

THE STREETS BLEED MURDER **I, II & III**

THE HEART OF A GANGSTA I & II

By **Jerry Jackson**

250

CUM FOR ME

CUM FOR ME 2

CUM FOR ME 3

An **LDP Erotica Collaboration**

BRIDE OF A HUSTLA **I & II**

THE FETTI GIRLS **I, II& III**

By **Destiny Skai**

WHEN A GOOD GIRL GOES BAD

By **Adrienne**

A GANGSTER'S REVENGE **I II III & IV**

THE BOSS MAN'S DAUGHTERS

THE BOSS MAN'S DAUGHTERS II

THE BOSSMAN'S DAUGHTERS III

A SAVAGE LOVE **I & II**

BAE BELONGS TO ME

A HUSTLER'S DECEIT I, II

By **Aryanna**

A KINGPIN'S AMBITON

A KINGPIN'S AMBITION **II**

I MURDER FOR THE DOUGH

By **Ambitious**

TRUE SAVAGE

TRUE SAVAGE II

TRUE SAVAGE **III**

By **Chris Green**

Coffee

A DOPEBOY'S PRAYER

By **Eddie "Wolf" Lee**

THE KING CARTEL **I, II & III**

By **Frank Gresham**

THESE NIGGAS AIN'T LOYAL **I, II & III**

By **Nikki Tee**

GANGSTA SHYT **I II &III**

By **CATO**

THE ULTIMATE BETRAYAL

By **Phoenix**

BOSS'N UP **I , II & III**

By **Royal Nicole**

I LOVE YOU TO DEATH

By Destiny J

I RIDE FOR MY HITTA

I STILL RIDE FOR MY HITTA

By **Misty Holt**

LOVE & CHASIN' PAPER

By **Qay Crockett**

TO DIE IN VAIN

By **ASAD**

BROOKLYN HUSTLAZ

By **Boogsy Morina**

BROOKLYN ON LOCK I & II

By **Sonovia**

Love Knows No Boundaries

GANGSTA CITY

By **Teddy Duke**

A DRUG KING AND HIS DIAMOND

A DOPEMAN'S RICHES

By Nicole Goosby

BOOKS BY LDP'S CEO, CA$H

TRUST IN NO MAN

TRUST IN NO MAN 2

TRUST IN NO MAN 3

BONDED BY BLOOD

SHORTY GOT A THUG

THUGS CRY

THUGS CRY 2

THUGS CRY 3

TRUST NO BITCH

TRUST NO BITCH 2

TRUST NO BITCH 3

TIL MY CASKET DROPS

RESTRAINING ORDER

RESTRAINING ORDER 2

IN LOVE WITH A CONVICT

Coming Soon

BONDED BY BLOOD 2

BOW DOWN TO MY GANGSTA

Love Knows No Boundaries